They stared at each other in amazement

Then Priscilla said stupidly, "You're not the horrible Barnabas?"

His lips tightened. "I am. Peter Barnabas Lockhart. And what the hell are you doing in my aunt's house when you told me you were in Christchurch? You lied to me. I thought I could trust you."

There just wasn't any answer to that. Priscilla thought tears would overwhelm her. He held up his hand. "Please, no tears. They'd have no effect on me."

Priscilla was suddenly filled with rage, and was glad. It was better than feeling guilty because she'd deceived him. And she couldn't let him know her feelings for him. She said hotly, "I can well believe that – after the experience you've had with other women!"

OTHER
Harlequin Romances
by ESSIE SUMMERS

My Lady of the Fuchsias

by

ESSIE SUMMERS

Harlequin Books

TORONTO • LONDON • NEW YORK • AMSTERDAM
SYDNEY • HAMBURG • PARIS

Original hardcover edition published in 1979
by Mills & Boon Limited

ISBN 0-373-02281-6

Harlequin edition published September 1979

To Sally Daley,
now of Napier, New Zealand,
but formerly of London,
who shares her three grandchildren with us,
and whose friendship we value.

The author wishes to record her thanks to
The Australian Woman's Mirror
for permission to use
Sonia Hardie's poem "Planning."

Printed in U.S.A.

CHAPTER ONE

PRISCILLA MARCHANT wondered later if, had the events of that day occurred weeks apart, she would ever have had the courage to turn her job in. She had lived cautiously for so long, because so much had depended upon her, that either she had acted out of character or had reverted to the kind of person she really was at heart.

More years of devotion to duty lay behind her than was the usual lot of twenty-seven-year-olds, especially for one who had been regarded as an afterthought in the family. Youngest children, born after a long gap, were often regarded as likely to be spoiled brats, or, at best, pampered. But it had been the young Priscilla who had to do the pampering after their father had died and her mother had become so dependent upon her.

Andrew, her brother, would have shouldered more of it and even offered to forgo his Nuffield scholarship and stay in New Zealand, but Priscilla wouldn't hear of it. 'Of course I can manage. I know Mother's delicate, but she's not an invalid.' She and Andrew had both looked away. They had known their mother was merely a *malade imaginaire*, but some innate sense of loyalty (or foolishness) kept them from admitting it, even to each other.

Andrew had said, 'It may be that she'll buck up now, without Dad to lean on. I've known cases like this. The prop's removed, and suddenly the bereft one finds she—or he—can cope, finds new strength.' It was the nearest to criticism they'd ever come, for they loved their mother in spite of her demands.

Andrew had added, 'And perhaps now Clarice will learn to stand on her own feet. Priscilla, you've just got to make her realise you can't be forever baby-sitting and gardening and ironing for her while she and Geoff gad. You'll have our garden on your own now—Mother's no gardener. And while I'm fond of Geoff, he does spoil Clarice, same as Mother always did. It makes me cross the way he turns to you when Clarice can't cope. This will do them all the good in the world—knowing you won't have the same time. It would have been far better when they married, if he had taken that transfer to Auckland and left Dunedin. But no, Clarice wanted to be near Mother.'

Priscilla had known her greatest wrench would be in parting with her brother, but she had never regretted it. Otherwise, his mother would have clung so much, he might never have married. Research in the medical field was undoubtedly what he had been destined for and his was a fine service to humanity. He had married a lovely girl, settled in Oxford, and came home on visits. His long and regular letters to Priscilla never failed to inspire and comfort her.

But the last five years hadn't been easy, even though she had had her own small satisfying joys. It had been worse, of course, when Geoffrey died so suddenly and Clarice hadn't even tried to cope. It had been a mistake, in the first flush of their sympathy for her, to build themselves a unit in the grounds of her home, with Clarice and her mother forever comforting each other, and looking to Priscilla to accomplish all her father had once done.

When her mother died, Priscilla made a bid to get away, but Clarice had promptly taken to her bed and Jill and Robin had had such a thin time of it that Priscilla had capitulated.

Just when Priscilla had become secretary to P. B. Lockhart of Lockhart's Department Store, Clarice had married again. It wouldn't have looked good on a reference had she left a firm so quickly and sought a position in another city, so now she had been with the firm for a year, and Clarice and Roger had been married eight months. Roger was a fine stepfather, and very good with Clarice, not indulgent, but loving and understanding.

Now, however, Priscilla knew it would have been wiser to have risked making a move then. How corny a situation to fall in love with one's boss and to know him to be emotionally involved with another woman, especially a fascinating, wilful creature like Melisande Drew. It had seemed particularly unbearable today. Melisande had been in twice, interrupting their work considerably till even Mr Lockhart sounded exasperated.

'Melisande, off with you. I'll see you tomorrow.'

She had pouted. 'Darling, why? What's the use of being a boss if you're still tied to a timetable? I'm sure the so-efficient Miss Marchant is both right and left hands to you. Come and have some afternoon tea in the restaurant.'

He'd said, 'I'll tell you why ... first because it's only a short time since I finished my business lunch, second because I find you distract me, third because Miss Marchant departs on holiday tomorrow, and I'll be stuck with that dilly Miss Freeman, and we must get on. Tomorrow, I said. Goodbye for now.'

Melisande reached up, kissed his square chin lightly, departed laughing.

Mr Lockhart said feelingly, 'There are times when I could smack her bottom.'

Priscilla didn't deign to reply. Her boss looked at her and sighed. 'Miss Marchant, sometimes your cool, impersonal attitude towards me riles me beyond bearing. I'm perfectly aware you'd like to say: "Well, why don't you?" I've never felt so much under the mantle of anyone's disapproval as I have with you. You're practically a slave-driver. I'm always on the verge of apologising to you when any friend drops in and work gets interrupted. There ... I've said what I've been wanting to say for ages! Not that you'll even flare up about that. Your emotions and your mind are as tidy as your files!'

Priscilla snapped the page out of her typewriter, swung her chair round, stood up. Her brown cheeks rarely showed much colour, but they were scarlet now. Her temper was red-hot.

'Mr Lockhart! When Miss Wincombe engaged me, she made it very plain to me that you preferred your secretaries to keep their distance . . . that in the past, as a very eligible bachelor, you'd suffered from the girlie types. You can't have it all ways, can you? How completely illogical! I thought I was fulfilling your requirements to the letter.'

He looked startled, then grinned. 'Touché . . . mind you, I didn't go as far as that with old Win. I just told her——'

He was interrupted. 'You probably told her to go for the plain and sensible type who wouldn't get ideas. Don't bother to spare my feelings—just admit it. I can take it. Only having got exactly what you wanted, I'm now getting on your nerves for being just that!'

He burst out laughing. 'My dear Miss Marchant! How truly absurd! Sensible, yes, for which I'm devoutly glad, but how could plain possibly apply to you? You've got that sort of brown elegance that grows on one. I only said to old Win that I didn't want a silly bit of fluff with ideas about marrying the boss and none whatever about deportment and filing.'

Because Priscilla knew only too well her feelings about P. B. Lockhart, she let her voice sound contemptuous. 'So . . . you got an elegant brown secertary, reasonably efficient with filing and typing and shorthand, able to deport herself with your business associates in a becoming manner, evidently, and certainly without ideas of marrying her boss. And what happens? You seem to resent her impersonal attitude. Does it pique your masculine ego? Does it mean you really like your secretaries to fall under your charm? You can't have it both ways, Mr Lockhart! However, if after a year of me, you find it boring and would rather have a bit of fluff, just tell me and I'll look elsewhere. One job's as good as another to me.'

Suddenly she felt that this would be the right moment to get away from all the complexes that were building up within her because of working at close quarters with a man who disturbed her as this man did and who, while not

—quite—engaged, undoubtedly soon would be.

Her chief stopped grinning and looked appalled. He came across to her, grabbed her by the elbow, said, 'Priscilla ... don't be such an idiot! Yes, I've called you Priscilla despite the fact that you informed me coolly the first time I did it that you'd always found it good policy to remain on formal terms with employers, but it's a beautiful name and I'm using it from now on.'

Priscilla said, 'I don't care what you call me. You can just say: "Here you," if you like! In actual fact, I doubt I'll be here much longer for you to call me anything. This isn't sudden, only triggered off by what you've just said. All sorts of plans have been going round in my head for long enough about my future. My emotions mightn't be half as tidy as you seem to think they are. My feelings have been most chaotic for some time, but naturally I've not allowed them to interfere with my work. This could be as good a time as any to tell you that during my holidays I'll probably be looking for another position up north. I'd return to work out my notice, of course, but my time here is definitely short.'

The square, lightly tanned face above hers changed completely. His voice held a blend of dismay and anger. 'Oh, come, surely to goodness you didn't have to take my remarks as seriously as that. I've never been so happy with a secretary. In every way you suit me. Look, I didn't mean to imply that you were a cold sort of female—I realise now that would put any girl's back up. I just meant why were you so stiff and starchy with me? Old Win certainly had put her foot in it. If I lose you as a secretary it'll ruin my present satisfaction. You've no idea how much you've taken off my shoulders. That's why you got upped in your pay packet three months ago. Now, you remember your boss's peace of mind and simmer down.'

Priscilla's voice was biting. 'And I suppose *your* peace of mind is all that matters?'

He groaned. 'What's the matter with me? I'm as bad as

Win—I just put my foot in it all the time. If only that phone would ring and save me, then you might cool off. Just imagine ... I was accusing you of being too impersonal, and you suddenly erupted. It's like picking up a comet by the tail and not being able to let go, and sailing across the sky with it, willy-nilly.'

Priscilla's brown eyes caught his blue ones, held them, and it was no good. Her mouth crumbled at the corners and laughter had its way with her. Her boss looked most relieved, caught her by the elbows again and said, 'Thank goodness you've got a sense of humour.' He started to laugh himself. 'Is it all over?'

She nodded. 'And at least I'll be away a couple of weeks. I'll probably wonder what came over me.'

'Good girl.' He released her. 'I'll enjoy working with you even more when you get back ... now I know you're human.'

Priscilla said crisply, 'I'll start those departmental reports. They're fairly routine, and even in my shattered state I should be able to get on with them.'

'Will you cope better if I retire to the Sanctum? I've a fair bit to do myself and with luck, now I've disposed of Melisande for the afternoon, I'll be able to concentrate. She's on duty tonight. Just as well, when it's late shopping night.'

'Duty? You mean she works? I thought she was——'

He cocked a tawny brow at her. 'You thought she was just a lily-of-the-field? I don't blame you.'

She made a rueful sound. 'Did you say *you* kept putting your foot in it? It must be catching. Just that she's so often in here at odd hours.'

'Oh, much more to Mel than looks and frivolity. She's a sort of Scarlet Pimpernel person. That froth and bubble air is the result of being spoiled. Beneath that she's a real person, like her grandmother, who was a fine old lady. She's a technician at Saint Monica's Hospital. Does shift work, of course, that's why she appears at leisure while most folk work.'

Priscilla was just recovering from her surprise when a tap sounded at the door and in response to Mr Lockhart's 'Come in,' her brother-in-law walked in.

She said, 'Oh, Roger, is anything wrong? Or——'

He said apologetically towards her chief, 'Mr Lockhart, I wonder if you'd be so good as to spare your secretary to me for about ten minutes or so? I just have to see her. I could perhaps take her to the restaurant—I'd appreciate that very much.'

Mr Lockhart said, 'I can do better than that. I'll offer you the privacy of my inner office.'

Roger demurred, naturally. 'Oh, I couldn't possibly do that, Mr Lockhart. I feel badly enough about coming in as it is, but with my sister-in-law off on holiday tomorrow, this was my one chance.'

Priscilla looked alarmed. What could he mean? Couldn't he have seen her tonight?

The chief was smilingly insisting. 'I just this moment put my big clumsy foot in it with my secretary and I'd like to make amends, so do let me. I'll bring my work out here and keep the telephone at bay.'

Priscilla felt unreal. For twelve months she'd worked on a most formal footing here and all in the space of twenty minutes or so seemed to have got on to a different one altogether.

Her boss ushered them into the Sanctum, picked up a wad of papers, switched the phone back to the outer office, and went to the door. He looked back over his shoulder and said solemnly, 'Anyway, Priscilla, I *have* done it.'

Priscilla said faintly, 'Done what?'

His eyes danced. 'Smacked Melisande's bottom . . .' then he added, 'Though I admit she was only eight.' He closed the door.

Roger Whitfield looked amazed. 'What an odd conversation to be having with one's boss. You're a dark horse. You said he kept things on a strictly formal footing, that it suited you very well. Clarice and I imagined him at least sixty, and quite a curmudgeon. But——'

'Well, it was that way, till half an hour ago or less, when we had a flaming row. We were just finished when you walked in and he's made this gesture because he thought I was going to hand in my notice. Seemingly he appreciates my services. What is it, Roger?'

'Thought you were going to hand in your notice? Seriously?'

For one crazy moment she thought Roger looked ... well ... eager? But how could that be? No, it must be some other emotion. He asked, 'How did he get that idea? How far did you go, Pris?'

'I told him one job was much like any other to me and I was seriously thinking of a change. Though it was only because I was so mad with him.'

'But you mean you aren't really wedded to this job. Have you anything in mind?'

'You mean something I've seen advertised? No. But I might——'

'You see, Priscilla, I just wondered if, at your age, you mightn't like to get away as so many single girls do and see a bit of the world? Good typists can get jobs anywhere and I'd not blame you. I know you couldn't very well when Clarice was on her own, but now it's different. When I had that trip to London and ran up to Oxford to meet Andrew, he said to me that it was time you lived your own life. He'd like to see you pull up the pegs. Why not? You could let your unit and junket round the world a bit. The rent would give you a certain income.'

Priscilla blinked. 'But, Roger, was it necessary to come to tell me this today? In my place of business?'

His jaw went a little grim. 'It was. I didn't want to risk Clarice walking in on us when I was putting it to you. No, don't look like that. I don't mean I want you out of it ...

off the property. This is for *your* sake, Pris. Andrew only confirmed what I'd suspected for myself . . . that you've had a pretty raw deal for long enough. Clarice has got to stop leaning on her younger sister. She's spoiling your life and warping her own nature in so doing.

'I don't want a clinging vine for a wife, always pitying herself. Andrew told me your mother was a bit of hypochondriac and that if I didn't watch it, Clarice would turn the same way. I know this may sound awful, but in some ways, she enjoyed being a widow and having people sorry for her. Well, she's not a widow any longer and she's damned well got to snap out of it. I won't have her imposing on you indefinitely.

'I've been biding my time and have come to the conclusion that if you don't make a break for it soon you'll always be tied to her. Oh, I'm not entirely motivated for your sake. It's for myself too. I've noticed how much the youngsters run to you for comfort, for advice, even for companionship and understanding. Clarice is less than a mother to them. Jill is already fetching and carrying too much for her mother.

'It got me today. I was home for lunch. Clarice calmly said, "Darling, you know Prissie is off on holiday, but hasn't any firm bookings . . . just having the weekend at Karitane and then going on to stay with that Christchurch friend and roaming round from there? And that she hopes to have a bash at writing a few short stories while her friend's at work? Well, I just thought if I accompanied you to Auckland next week, she could stay on here and write them just as well; the children would have her to come home to, and I could shop while you called on your clients." '

Roger grinned a little. 'I'm afraid I blew up—said it just wasn't going to happen, that I wasn't selfish enough to expect my sister-in-law to give up a holiday so we could be together. But I know what it's going to be. She'll let hints drop, hoping you'll offer just that. And I won't be in till late tonight. I thought I'd come home to find it all settled. And I won't have it. Don't mistake me, I love Clarice, but I want Clarice the way she ought to be, and that's a mature and lovely woman, not a petulant child. So, Pris, don't come back after your weekend at Karitane. Drive on north. You need a life of your own. Clarice doesn't need you any more. She's got a husband and children, and if you get away from us you'll probably acquire the same within a year. I know there've been a few who'd have liked to fill the bill, but I can imagine most men would hesitate about taking on a wife at the beck and call of an entire family. Hey, Pris, steady on . . . what is it? Have I sounded a bit brutal? As if you weren't wanted? I didn't mean that—it's just I can't stand seeing anyone not get a fair deal.'

He took her by the upper arms, gazed into her tear-filled eyes. 'I've never once seen you cry, and Clarice sheds quarts.'

She shook her head, impatiently dashing at her eyes, then was offered his handkerchief. 'It's not that, Roger. You're the dearest person. It's just that I've never had anyone do as much for me before—or since Andrew went away. So it got me.' She mopped up.

Roger said, 'You've said so little about your job here I'd an idea you didn't care for it much, but with a boss like that, you'd not want to leave, but if you stay on with him, you ought to find yourself another flat so you're not at your sister's beck and call all day—well, at nights and weekends! Why don't you let yours and take one at St Clair, or Halfway Bush or somewhere? As far from Pine Hill as possible? Then you could start living your own life.'

She smiled at him a little mistily, took a few steps towards the door, turned the handle, then with it a little ajar turned back to him and said, 'I'll do just that, Roger. I think neither of us would want to carry on like this. The only thing would be what you said, a clean break. We ought never to have let it develop into a situation like this.' They walked out into the outer office.

Mr Lockhart looked extremely busy at Priscilla's desk.

His face when he did look up was expressionless. He nodded casually to Roger. Priscilla said, 'I've just realised I didn't introduce you. This is Roger Whitfield, my brother-in-law. And of course, Roger, you know this is my chief, Mr Peter Lockhart.'

For once Mr Lockhart's urbanity seemed to have deserted him. He appeared ill at ease. 'Yes, I thought he said you were his sister-in-law.' Then he stopped, appeared to search for words, but apparently found none. Priscilla had a feeling his tone had been one of surprise. Why?

Roger said, 'Well, I can't thank you enough for sparing her and offering us your office, especially when I imagine you're clearing up some last-minute things before she goes on holiday.'

Mr Lockhart nodded. 'Yes, but she's been flat out all day. We aren't too rushed, you were welcome.'

Just as Roger departed, Priscilla realised she still had his handkerchief. She went after him to the door, pushed it into his hand and as she turned back, found Peter Lockhart's eyes fixed upon her, a frown between his brows. She felt embarrassed and flushed.

He got up, merely said brusquely, 'Right, now let's return to normal.' She felt guilty, as if she'd wasted time, then annoyed, because after all, he'd offered her that time. But she contented herself with sitting down, saying, 'By the way, if we don't get through, I could work on. I'm just going as far as Karitane tomorrow, and I've all evening to pack.'

'It won't be necessary,' said her boss, and disappeared into his own office.

Priscilla disciplined her disturbed thoughts. She mustn't dwell on what Roger had said, in business hours. Time enough to mull it over tonight. One thing she knew ... there was going to be a big change in her life. This was evidently the tide to be taken at the full. Roger felt it was best for her to go, and he'd done it in kindly fashion. But there was nothing to be gained by getting a flat in another suburb and continuing to work here in close proximity to Peter Lockhart.

She'd go on up to Christchurch and look for a job there. She divorced her mind from dwelling on that and worked on. The mail was despatched, certain things checked, instructions given to the dilly Miss Freeman, and it was time for the tea-hour break at six for herself and her boss. They would return at seven and work till eight-thirty like the shop assistants. She was just picking up her bag when she heard her chief utter a dismayed exclamation. She called out, 'What is it, Mr Lockhart? Anything I can do?'

He appeared in the doorway, his jacket in his hands, drawing out a bundle of letters. Not business ones, for sure. He said, 'I was going to have these despatched by the first mail this morning. I wanted them delivered tomorrow.'

'I'll post them now, that should get them there. Oh, are they not for Dunedin?'

'That's the trouble. Not that they're far away, but almost all on rural mail delivery, I don't think there's a hope. I can't deliver them personally tonight, and I'm boxed in tomorrow. It's Horticultural Society stuff, something I planned myself, and I thought the people concerned could get cracking on this experiment tomorrow. Blast it! They're away out on the Taieri Plain in the Fair-acre Valley area.'

Priscilla found herself offering immediately. 'Mr Lockhart, I've finished everything necessary. Miss Freeman can cope with what's left. I know you can't be away late shopping night, but I could do this for you. I can't think of anything more pleasant in this long February twilight than driving round the Taieri. I've a rural map of that area in my car—I mean, with all the names of the homesteads marked.'

He laughed. 'Your efficiency leaves me gasping. How come you carry a map like that? How many people would?'

The brown eyes facing him went a little sombre. 'My brother-in-law—not the one you met but my sister's first husband—was in Governmental experimental work and I used to do a lot of his correspondence. I've got maps of most areas round here. One even of north of Dunedin with your own estate marked . . . Tyne Hill.'

'My father's estate. Of course you've not been here in his time. I've globe-trotting parents. They've been away nearly two years. Not that I grudge them a minute of it. They worked like Trojans in their young days.'

'But you live there and manage it, I believe?'

'I do while they're away, but only till they come back.'

She felt she was getting too personal. He was meaning till he got married, she supposed. She said, 'How about it? Or would you prefer me to work on here?'

He considered it. 'It would help tremendously if you'd do it. But it could mean you'll be even later than if you stayed here and I expect you have to pack. I was thinking of telling you to push off early.'

'I can pack tomorrow morning.'

He accepted her offer. She said, 'That'll give me nearly three hours till nine anyway, and it's not dark till ten with daylight saving.'

He said, 'Three hours? That means you're planning to skip your meal. Oh, no, Miss Marchant, I'll take you to the restaurant now.'

'No, that'll delay me. I'll snatch a sandwich at the cafeteria.'

'I don't think you would. You'd just go.'

'I promise I'll have a sandwich, but a meal at the restaurant would take too long to serve.'

He grinned, 'Right, but I'll come with you to make sure.'

'Oh, Mr Lockhart, it's not done for the boss to eat there.'

'Oh, bosh. Then it's time it was done. Didn't I often eat there when I was learning the trade? I may seem like the boss now, but once I was just a staff member. Come on and don't argue.'

It was just as she'd expected, the moment the boss pushed the swing doors open, the free buzz of conversation ceased. He laughed, one brow cocked quizzically in Priscilla's direction, 'I see what you mean. I'm inhibiting them, aren't I?' He swung back from the counter, tray in hand, waved a hand at the tables, said clearly, 'Everyone relax . . . I'm eating here to save time. Don't let it give you indigestion.'

They all laughed and resumed eating or munching. He ordered salmon mayonnaise with crisp lettuce curls for them, brown bread-and-butter, cheese and biscuits and tea. He'd ordered a large pot and drank three cups, so Priscilla spent longer over the meal than she had meant to. She thought he was doing it purposely to relax her. He leafed over the envelopes with her, giving her a rough idea of the sequence of delivery that would make it easier for her.

He said, 'I've a good mind to turn it in tonight and come with you. I could drive and you could just slip out with the envelopes at each gate.'

It tempted her, but she turned it down. It would have been something to remember . . . riding with him in the late summer twilight in the green-meadowed peace of the Taieri Plain close up against the Maungatuas, rising gently from the pastures, sweet with pockets of native bush, melodious with birdsong and rippling rivulets, and with a sunset sky to stain the clouds with lavish colours.

'I offered to do it to save your time, Mr Lockhart.'

'So you did. You keep me on the rails, don't you? I'm not to waste time.' She didn't answer. He drank his last mouthful of tea, put his cup down, leaned across to her, said in a low voice, 'I think you want to be on your own, don't you, my stiff-and-starchy-but-suddenly-human secretary? You have things to think over, to decide, I gather?'

She felt a little alarmed, hesitated.

He said, 'I couldn't help overhearing a little. Oh, not all, just at the last when you opened the door. I was sorry. I —well, I suppose these situations can occur. You seemed to be taking the right line. You've decided to break away?'

Her voice was just as low. 'Yes, it's the only thing. Harm has already been done. Only it won't be easy.'

'I know, but if you're convinced it's right it's often

easier than you think. Life can take on a new pattern, a new direction.' The blue eyes lit up. 'I sound like my own grandfather! Must be the employer syndrome. Hard to resist saying: "Let's know if I can do anything," but if having three weeks instead of a fortnight's holiday would help, I'll make do with the dilly Miss Freeman for an extra week.'

He didn't know what he was doing to Priscilla. He was so—so understanding. She said crisply, 'I appreciate that very much, but I had my other week earlier when Clarice wasn't well. But thank you. I'll manage fine.'

He said, 'My apologies for being so cutting today about your emotional attitude. I accused you of being cool and impersonal, not letting yourself go, and all the time you were coping with a situation like this. How superficial many of our judgments are! Well, it's not exactly the moment for wishing you a happy holiday in these circumstances, but . . . don't brood too much. Have a jolly good time as far as you can. How do you intend to make this break?'

She felt she couldn't mention a break with Dunedin, with her job, right now. She said, 'As I think you know, my mother and I had a unit built on part of my sister's property. I kept it on after Mother died, but it was a mistake. It meant we saw too much of each other. I'll get one further away. That's as much as I can decide for the moment. I'll make the break not too dramatically—for Roger's sake.' She rose as he pulled out her chair for her and walked to the door with him, watched by the interested eyes of about thirty per cent of the staff. They parted at the door leading to the staff parking lot.

The sunset and the twilight were all she could have wished. She took Three-Mile Hill, dipping through the groves of larch and birch and fir, then emerging to see the plain spread out before her in its chequer-board of green and gold fields, many ripening now to harvest, and intersected with the silver gleam of waters taking their way to the Pacific.

The cool air fanned her cheeks and brow, giving her an illusion of peace and well-being. Sleek-flanked dairy herds grazed and white-woolled sheep. As she went over the bridge across the Taieri River at Outram Glen, parents were watching over children splashing in the shallows.

Priscilla envied them. Their lives were settled, happy ... well, most of them would be happy, she hoped. To be loved, to have a home of one's own, to have children as a pledge of continuing life, a sort of immortality ... these were the things most women still longed for. Not the only things in life, because a taste of career life before marriage and the knowledge that one could make one's own way was very satisfying, but marriage crowned it all.

She found all sorts of little roads and lanes not known before, and noticed many of the farmhouses were out of sight of their mailboxes at the gates. She left the letters for the Fair-acre Valley village till the last. She hadn't been there for years and had forgotten how beautiful it was. It had more of the village atmosphere than most New Zealand townships. Perhaps because it was on no main highway, but nestled back into its glen, content with its own existence, dreamy and slow-paced, yet with such easy access to a city like Dunedin.

The membership of the Horticultural Society was certainly a cross-section of the community here ... the butcher, the baker, the candlestick-maker (well, the electrician) a poultry farmer, the doctor's, the Manse. All had lovely gardens. Only one letter left. It lay a little out of the village, in a road that first skirted the river, then wound round a hill. It was really a tree-girt lane, with more of a track than a footpath.

She turned the corner and there it was, with a high brick wall in front of it. She glanced at the name on the wrought iron gate, and checked it with the last envelope. Yes, Mrs M. Claremont, Jesmond Dene, Larchwood Road, Fair-acre Valley. What a lovely address! That letter was thicker than the others. Perhaps there was a flower catalogue in it. She went across to the mailbox. From the colourful glimpse of that garden through the wrought-iron gate it was certainly a garden-lover who lived here. As she turned to cross back to her car, her attention was caught by a peculiarity of the brick wall. The rest of its curve was perfectly symmetrical, but suddenly it bent back and made a half loop round a chestnut tree of magnificent size and round the trunk was an octagonal seat that positively invited one to sit on it. And why not? From now on she was on holiday.

It was evident from the two shades of the bricks that someone had actually made a gap in the wall so it could be taken back behind the tree. What an enchanting idea, to share the shade with passers-by.

How long Priscilla sat there dreaming, she didn't know. She was only dimly conscious of a hundred scents from behind the wall and a thrush's cascading song from the tip of a poplar, and daisies and clover at her feet.

Suddenly she heard a dismayed yell from in the garden, and then a woman's voice, thoroughly exasperated, 'Hell and damnation! That *would* have to happen. I'll never be able to get down. But I'll give it a darned good try . . . or that horrible Barnabas will say: "What *did* I tell you?" Ohh!'

It sounded as if the owner of the voice was gnashing her teeth. Priscilla knew she would have to investigate. She hadn't heard a crash, but it was ten to one that a ladder had fallen and someone was treed. Heaven send she could get there before any bones were broken. Priscilla ran.

CHAPTER TWO

As she tore through the gates and up the flanks of fuchsias on the drive she was calling out: 'Where are you? Can I help?' over and over again, pausing for an answer.

Whoever was in trouble must have got such a shock at instant succour, for there was no reply immediately; then it came. 'Over here in the shrubbery, there's a path.' Priscilla dived along it, guided by the voice at intervals, reached a huge Wellingtonia, and peered up into it. She distinguished a little old lady high up, dangling from a branch by the hem of her frock so that spindly little legs swung below her well-exposed underwear.

She choked back a laugh in the nick of time. 'How on earth did you get up there? No, don't answer that. Just hang on. I'll climb up to you.'

She wished she'd had trousers on, or even a shorter and wider skirt, but she managed it, tearing tights and scratching her legs as she went quickly up through the bristly branches she used as steps. One consolation, Wellingtonias were so thick with branches there was no dangerous reaching from one to the next.

She reached a level with the little figure and was surprised to find it shaking with the giggles. A pair of mischievous hazel eyes gazed into hers. 'I can't believe my incredible luck ... to have someone find me so soon. And a woman at that. The minister's coming over lateish tonight and I'd just as soon it wasn't him to rescue me.'

Priscilla had wedged her feet firmly so could reach out to hold her. 'I should have thought you'd not have cared had it been the archangel Gabriel himself, as long as someone got you down! What on earth possessed you to climb a tree at your age?'

Dimples appeared. 'It was Barnabas's fault really—my nephew. I'm taking some relatives while their parents are in Papua, and he said I wasn't to, that I hadn't the sense I was born with. That I'd try to keep up with them, and he wouldn't put it past me to go climbing trees with them and break my neck. I felt mad with him for about two whole days and tonight I was peering up at a darling tomtit in this tree and thought what an easy one to climb and I'd go clean to the top, then ring him up and tell him the tallest tree in the garden is nothing to me.'

Priscilla couldn't help a small giggle herself. 'And you got hooked! Maybe this Barnabas knows a thing or two. Now look, if I push your knees up, you can get your feet resting on two small branches, enough to take the weight off your dress, then I'll climb up past you and either hook it off or tear it off. But you'll have to cling to me while I push you or you'll slip.'

'What a really resourceful girl you are! You must come in and have a cup of tea and tell me about yourself when we get down, dear.' It sounded so perfectly ordinary it gave Priscilla an odd feeling as if anything could be accepted as the norm in this enchanted garden.

She said, 'Now . . . . move this foot to the left, and up a wee bit . . . oh, that's good. Now, bend the other knee so I can push that one a bit higher . . . ah! Now, shrink against the tree so I can pass you . . . good girl . . . what a blessing you're so tiny and I'm a beanpole. Hold firmly now, while I edge past.'

Even with the weight taken off the material, it was very firmly hooked on and was very tough crimplene. Finally Priscilla had to exert real pressure to snap the thick twig and the little lady was free. Priscilla said hastily, 'Don't you dare start climbing down. I'll pass you again, then if you fall you'll fall on me.'

'Oh, dear, you sound just like Barnabas. Just because I'm in my seventies, only my mid-seventies, mark you, people think I'm feeble. I can run rings round most of them.'

'I'm sure you can, but don't let's give the said Barnabas any justification for saying: "I told you so." There, I'm past you. Edge down from one branch to another.'

They were almost down when it happened. The little lady stepped on to a branch Priscilla had avoided. It was too light even for her. She fell on Priscilla, who tried to clutch her with one hand and cling to a good hold with the other, but it took her off balance and they both crashed to the ground. It was a short distance by then and they landed on a cushiony bed of pine-needles blown from a clump some distance away.

Just as the little lady was trying to scramble off Priscilla a voice said, 'What on earth are you up to now, Rosina?'

It would be the horrible Barnabas. What beastly timing! Priscilla was flat on her back but raised her head and looked straight at a broad, fair man, wearing a dog collar. Heavens, the parish minister, come early! She said, 'Thank goodness it's not Barnabas!'

He grinned. 'I should think you *would* give thanks that it isn't Barnabas. What on earth are you doing encouraging Rosina to climb trees? She's mad enough without the younger generation egging her on.'

Priscilla, a little winded from having Rosina crash on her, struggled to a sitting-up position and was about to hotly disclaim any egging-on when Rosina, laughing helplessly, did it for her. 'Dougal MacNab, don't jump to conclusions. This young lady rescued me. She must have been passing by and heard me. Otherwise I'd have been hanging there still ... I was hooked on by my hem, and really, to have my minister climb up to rescue me, with my skirt above my head, would have been too, too humiliating!'

He grinned, 'But much worse for me. I'd have caught your eye in church Sunday morning and burst out laughing. But why did you——'

'I was trying to prove to myself and Barnabas that I jolly well could still climb trees ... but it sort of staggered this young lady too. I say, I can't keep on referring to you as that. What is your name?'

'Priscilla Marchant. I was sitting on that lovely welcoming seat when I heard you . . . er . . . call out.'

'You mean when you heard me swear! Tell the truth and shame the devil. You won't shock the Reverend Mr McNab. I ought to formally introduce you . . .'

Priscilla said, 'I hardly think it's necessary. As an American friend of mine would say, we've gotten acquainted already.'

The minister hauled them to their feet, picking twigs off them. 'I wish I'd brought Elspeth along, but she was putting Scott and Jeannie down. They go off a bit later these light nights. How she'd have enjoyed seeing that heaving mass of bodies and limbs trying to sort itself out! But tell me, are you both all right? I can see scratches, but how about making sure you've not got sprained ankles or wrists? Rosina, I'll ring Mark and get him to give you the once-over. Miss Marchant, are——'

Rosina was indignant. 'It was nothing but a little tumble. We were almost down. Leave Mark be. Miss Marchant—oh, I can't keep calling you that after all this, Priscilla, how about you? After all, you cushioned my fall. Any bruises? Or worse? I'll make good the damage to your clothes, of course.'

'You will not,' said Priscilla firmly. 'For some ridiculous reason I've enjoyed it. I was feeling very staid and set in my ways and now I'm all shook up and feel about sixteen again.'

The minister grinned. 'Rosina has that effect on everyone. Eternally young. Though she constantly involves us in pranks. Come inside and I'll make the pair of you a cup of tea.'

They exchanged the usual small talk as they came out from the copsy corner. Priscilla said she lived in Dunedin and had just been out for a drive in the cool of the evening, saw the seat and couldn't resist sitting on it. She didn't mention delivering the notices. She'd left one at the manse, so this minister had probably met her chief at the Horti-cultural Society meetings. It could be a tale the minister would enjoy telling if he knew where she worked.

At the turn of the drive she saw the house for the first time and was enchanted. It was embowered in trees and was low and wide, timbered, and painted brown with white facings at the small-paned windows. The fuchsias bordered the drive right up to the house, in all their glowing reds and purples, pinks and whites, and the curved stone steps each had a mossy figure on them. Garden furniture on the wide porch looked inviting and creepers clung lovingly round posts and pillars.

Three little windows that looked like a cross between dormers and attics seemed to peer out from the steep roof and behind the house, above the notched outline of the tree-tops, was the slope of a hill and above it the tender primrose and green of a late evening sky.

Dougal MacNab seemed most domesticated and obviously knew the house well. He sent them off to wash their scratched hands, and by the time they returned had the tea set out in a pastel-tinted drawing-room that looked on a croquet lawn. Croquet! Priscilla felt as if she'd stepped back a generation. Though she believed it was enjoying a return to popularity. She had discarded her ruined tights and felt reasonably tidy again. Rosina Claremont had changed into a jersey silk dress as colourful as the fuchsias outside and her adventure didn't seem to have upset her in the slightest. She said so, sipping tea.

'Just the same,' said the minister reprovingly, 'you aren't spending the night alone here. If I went home without you and told Elspeth, she'd be over here like a lintie to get you.'

Rosina pulled a face at him. 'I so like my own bed, Dougal lad. It's doing me a kindness to stay here. Makes me feel my age if I have to be cosseted.'

He twinkled. 'That's a form of selfishness if you think

it over, this independence. It would worry us both, so for our peace of mind you must pick out your night-things and come. I'll run you back first thing tomorrow morning if you think Leonora or Sweet Annie or Victor Hugo will sicken and die without you.'

Priscilla looked all curious. 'What are they? Cats? Budgies? Can't be dogs, because they'd have barked.'

He burst out laughing. 'They're fuchsias, all named and precious. Each has a personality to Rosina. Most of her trees have names too, not just their botanical ones. I'm adamant about this, Rosina. You may as well give in graciously. I won't leave you alone tonight.'

Priscilla spoke before she thought. 'What say I stay the night?' Then she coloured up because it could be thought presuming. 'Oh, sorry. You wouldn't want some chance-met stranger in your home.'

Rosina looked at her, the hazel eyes wide and un-expectedly shrewd. 'You aren't chance-met. I think you were meant to come here at the very moment you did. Otherwise I might still be dangling and perhaps getting scared in spite of my bravado. It somehow turns a page back for me, you coming here because of the seat round the chestnut tree. It was Manuel's idea, you see. It's as if he was still taking care of me. His rustic bench lured you here when I needed you.'

Magic sent a tingling along Priscilla's wrists, a faint feathering of delight. That was the stuff dreams—and stories—were made of, woven right through what had been a very trying day. She looked across at the minister. 'What would you say? I don't think one should be too casual at accepting a person into one's home. I'm a member of St Adrian's Church, West Hill. You might like to check with Mr Smith, the minister there.'

He grinned. 'No need. You're what Elspeth calls "of the race that knows Joseph." So is Rosina. I'll be very happy to think of you staying with her tonight. Don't leave too early in the morning. I'll bring Elspeth round to meet you. It's

Saturday, so you won't be working, I take it?'

'No, and in any case I'm starting my holidays from to-night. I'm a typist in a Dunedin office and I'm having two weeks off.'

Rosina said, 'What time do you have to leave tomorrow? Would it hold you up?'

'No, I've all day tomorrow to prepare. I'm going on to stay at a friend's holiday house at Karitane the first night, on my own. Then on to stay with a friend in Christchurch. I'd love to stay if you lend me something to sleep in. I've a flat of my own, but I'll ring my sister next door to tell her where I am.'

The minister felt this was an ideal situation and began to depart. He looked down on his petite parishioner as she escorted him to the door, asked, 'How will you explain Miss Marchant if Barnabas rings?'

She pulled a face. 'He won't ring. He wrote me a letter two days ago and said he'll give me a week to think it over and expects me to have some horse-sense about it. That at my age I oughtn't to be so scatty, and that if at the end of the week I'm still determined to take the children, he's going to have something to say to their parents. That suited me fine—it gave me a breathing-space.' A gamin-like grin spread over the small, exquisite features. 'Because by the time his week is up, dear Barnabas won't be able to speak to Zillah and Keith. Their departure for Papua has been advanced and he doesn't know. So presented with a *fait accompli* he'll bow to the inevitable.'

Dougal MacNab shook his head over her and departed.

Rosina said, 'This is delightful. I'm so glad I got treed. I'm sure it was Fate. I can call you Priscilla, can't I? Such a beautiful name.'

'Of course you can, but never, never make it Prissie.'

'You don't mean anyone ever shortened it? How stupid! I know how you feel ... I had a grievance too, but in re-verse. I couldn't stand being called by my full name.'

'Which is?'

'It's a shocker. It's Ambrosina!'

They both giggled. Rosina looked appreciative. 'Oh, I do like you, Priscilla. You're a giggler like me. Doesn't it make life light-hearted? Even in sad moments, humour lights them. Were you a family of gigglers? It usually runs that way.'

'No. Dad and I and Andrew were blessed with an impish sense of humour that Clarice and Mother could rarely understand. They took life more seriously. My sister still does. I always have the feeling Clarice rather likes people to be sorry for her. Is that awful of me?'

'Not a bit. Some are born that way. Others get into the habit of it. In the end they're never happy unless they're miserable!'

This odd slant made Priscilla feel much happier about deserting Clarice. Her sister would moan for a bit about missing her, then learn to do things for herself. She certainly wouldn't like Priscilla taking a flat at some distant part of the same city. She'd say people would think they'd fallen out. Much better if Priscilla could find a job somewhere else. Better for herself too, to escape from the real pain of being secretary to a man to whom she meant little beyond a model of efficiency, a filing system, someone who kept interruptions away from his too-busy hours.

Rosina chatted on about her defiance of the formidable Barnabas. 'He said he'd not feel so strangely if I could get someone to help me, even part-time. Says it's one thing having the children here visiting me with their parents, and another having three high-spirited children all day and all night, on my own. But it will give Zillah such peace of mind to go with Keith. And him.'

A line appeared between Priscilla's brows. 'I'd have thought she'd have had less peace of mind leaving her children behind in New Zealand.' Maybe the horrible Barnabas was right. Perhaps Zillah wanted the good time of living in an exciting Pacific community. Free of the responsibility of children.

Rosina looked at her, then seemed to make up her mind.
'I can tell you the real reason because you don't know anyone concerned. Zillah didn't want it talked about, because
in the sort of post Keith is in, scandal can be quite ruinous.
I didn't tell Barnabas because he has such a scatty girl-
friend and she happens to know Keith's crowd quite well.
Keith hopes if he makes a success of this post in Papua,
with a sort of watching brief for New Zealand interests
there, it might be England next, and he's from there and it
would give his family the chance of getting to know their
grandchildren.

'He had three months in Papua last year and the daughter
of a contractor there, worth a mint of money and spoiled
as they come, made a dead set at him. Keith was only
terrified Zillah might get to hear of it and think the worst,
so he got her to fly in for the August school holidays with
the children, to stress the fact he was a married man.

'He felt he must have Zillah with him when he went back.
She's a real man-eater, this Hermia. She and I—Zillah, I
mean—have been very close, especially since my own
daughter went overseas. Her grandmother was like an
older sister to me. I owe her a terrific amount, and this is
one way I can repay that. Most of all, Zillah wants me to
have the children because I love and understand them. I believe in discipline, but the discipline of love. I agree I'm
going to get overtired, but if I could get the right person
to help, I'd take her. I couldn't pay much of a wage, so it
would have to be half-time.' At that moment the phone
rang. The instrument was in the drawing-room so Priscilla
heard it all.

Rosina said, 'Of course, Zillah. No trouble at all. As a
matter of fact, it will be better this way—not long enough
for the children to get all worked up. Besides, you know me,
I'm excited as a child myself. I'll love the company. I've got
the linen sorted already. I've a nice young friend staying the
night and she'll help me make up the beds first thing tomorrow.' She winked wickedly at Priscilla. 'I don't believe

you've met her. Just drop the children in and be on your way. If you leave your car here it will be quite safe. I'll drive you to the airport myself. Now off the phone and on with that packing. And Zillah, don't be disappointed if the children don't seem as upset as they should be. They love Jesmond Dene and will look on it as a holiday. I'll see they write once a week at least, and so will I. No, not another word. Off you go.'

She put the phone down, giggled. 'Poor Barnabas! Just as well he's letting me think it over. They're going sooner still. By the time he gets out here, they'll be so well established, he'll see there's no need to worry. You heard? They've been advised to leave right now, because if they reach Australia by a certain time they can get a connection which means they can go inland for some inspection work with an expedition that's setting off then. That's marvellous. Then this Hermia creature won't even see him!'

The attic bedroom she gave Priscilla was a delight, with an old-fashioned paper with purple and silver stripes, blue true lovers'-knots and little gilt cherubs scattered all over it. Clarice would have said, 'How too, too quaint,' but Priscilla loved it on sight. The bedspread was genuine patchwork, faded and worn into a harmonious whole, it had a newish pale grey carpet, a tiny desk, a chest of drawers and a wardrobe that sloped under the eaves. The window set in the roof pushed outwards and gazed into the copse over the brilliant heads of the fuchsias. The Wellingtonia stood guard over all. By now stars were beginning to prick out above the hill.

Priscilla said, 'How funny! This is the sort of place I thought existed only in dreams. I've the funniest feeling I've seen it before, but that's quite silly.'

Rosina shook her white head with its traces of chestnut. 'I still think it's a kind of recognition. Like people. You meet someone and you know you're on the right wavelength. You must come back after your holiday and get to know Jesmond Dene. Oh, I do wish you didn't have to go because——' she stopped, flushed, said, 'Oh, what a selfish thing for me to think, much less start to say.'

'But you will finish it, won't you?' begged Priscilla. 'Because if you say what I think you were going to say ... and wish I could stay on, oh, how I'd love to. I can stay with my friend in Christchurch any old time.'

The hazel eyes danced. 'Done! I should bleat I couldn't expect you to do it, but I won't. It's too providential.'

'I'd rather spend two weeks here than in a city,' said Priscilla. Then, 'Maybe Zillah would take more kindly to the idea if she went on believing I was a young friend of yours, or wouldn't you care to deceive her?'

'It's for her own peace of mind. We mustn't add to any doubts she already has. What a pity we don't have some mutual friends. I mean, if she thought you were somebody's niece, or cousin ... you said Marchant. You wouldn't be any relation of Seth Marchant? The late Seth Marchant? The lawyer?'

A light sprang into Priscilla's brown eyes. 'Did you know him? Know my father? Oh, it would be providential and rather heart-warming.'

Rosina said solemnly, 'This was foreordained ... that you should drop in on me tonight.'

Priscilla's lips twitched. 'I thought *you* dropped on *me*. How did you meet my father? He's been gone seven years.'

'He was my solicitor. It was a tragedy he died in his prime. Men of his calibre are so needed. But even Barnabas couldn't turn his nose up at Seth Marchant's daughter.'

What a bugbear this Barnabas was to his lovable aunt! Priscilla could well imagine him ... pompous, portly, prosperous. Heavens, what alliteration! He was more likely skinny, sarcastic, sneering. More alliteration. Just the sort to fall for a scatty girl-friend. No discrimination. They were the ones who liked the bits of fluff.

Her eyes fell on the nightgown Rosina had brought. She took it from her and shook it out. A shorty nightgown in cool dacron, lilac-sprigged. Obviously Rosina thought it would go with the wallpaper. She laughed, 'Dear Rosina, I said I was a beanpole . . . I'll just sleep in my petticoat.'

Rosina said she had a better idea and came back with a white cambric garment, with a square neck slotted through with pink ribbon, and long sleeves edged with embroidery. 'It was my mother's. She was tall and stately too. So was Father. Where they got a shrimp like me from I'll never know. Now, let's go and have a snack and look at some television, unless . . .' she put her head on one side and looked hopefully at Priscilla, 'unless you'd rather do a crossword with me. Or don't you?'

'I do. A crossword a day, that's me. Only I like help with them.'

'So do I. But you must ring your sister first in case she worries. Oh, isn't this delightful? What will you tell your sister?'

Priscilla considered. 'That I called here to ask directions and found an old friend of our father's. And you asked me to stay the night. Clarice is a conventional creature and would never understand about you having a sudden impulse to climb a tree.'

Priscilla woke with a sense of strangeness. Why were all these birds singing? It was like being in a wood. Where was she? Light filtered in slowly and made dancing leaf shadows on the sloping ceiling and already perfume drifted in at the open casement . . . oh, yes, she was at Jesmond Dene and beneath her window she'd noticed a mixed bed of Virginia and night-scented stock . . . the latter would be just closing, and the dew would accentuate its fragrance. She was going to be here for a blissful fortnight, free of all chores for Clarice, living with someone who had a light heart and a gay voice despite what must be great loneliness. Only you couldn't associate sadness with Rosina Claremont, only a sort of singing contentment with life as if the memories of her Manuel had sweetened the bitterness of bereavement.

She could hear Rosina stirring, so she must be up and doing too. A quick shower and she felt a giant refreshed. Rosina put Priscilla more in the picture as they breakfasted. The children's parents lived out on the plains on a ten-acre property so they already attended Fair-acre Valley School, so no problems there.

'Tell me about Nat and Tim's sister. You mentioned the boys last night, and they sounded like perfectly ordinary boys. But apart from saying Alicia is nine, I know nothing. Is she the quiet one? Or is it just that we associate any variant of the name of Alice with the Wonderland child with hair neatly banded back and a little precise in her manner?'

Rosina burst out laughing. 'She *does* have hair beneath an Alice-band, and she *is* very precise in her speech, but there it ends. She's a holy terror and I adore her. She's always in trouble through sheer goodness of heart, always fighting other people's battles and sponsoring lost causes. That's why I can't bear her to go to anyone else. I understand her.'

Priscilla was surprised to find herself giving Rosina a hug. 'Then I guess she's just like you. That's why this wretched Barnabas doesn't want you to have them. But we'll show him, won't we, that you, with some help from me, can cope? We'll get them well settled down in our week's grace, then I'll have another week with you after that.'

Rosina said wistfully, 'Then when you go back to work, would there be any chance of you coming out here at nights and weekends? Oh, dear, I shouldn't ask that.'

Priscilla said thoughtfully, 'It might be a good idea at that. I'm tired of living in town. I could let my flat for a few weeks. I work in an office from nine till five-thirty. I'm sure we could work something out. Now let's do the dishes.'

They made the beds. Rosina showed Priscilla a playroom her children had had, at the back of the house. It led out to a lawn where there was a sand-pit, a slide, and under a huge old willow, called Mammy, a big swing.

'Manuel said never to reconstruct this part of the garden. We could provide for children of all ages this way, and so recapture some of the lovely memories of the green years of our own children's lives ... and their children's children too, perhaps. They do come here, for their holidays. And this room, as I said to Barnabas when he was at his most horrible, makes having Zillah's children possible. Bless them, they can have it as their own domain and not be made to pick up their bits and pieces every meal-time.'

Priscilla looked round with appreciative eyes. 'I'd have loved this when I was small. Mother was so houseproud. Oh, I can't bear dirt and disorder, but there are limits. What treasures of books and games and old toys! Shall I flick a duster round?'

'No, let them do it. It will take their minds off their parents' going. Oh, I can hear a car.'

There was a gay tattoo on a horn, and out tumbled the family. Zillah's eyes were bright, too bright. Keith was being casual, too casual. This family circle was going to be broken for quite a time. Fortunately there was a terrific lot to do, carrying in of vast quantities of clothing, toys, sports equipment, books. Yards and yards of books.

Priscilla was amazed to see dolls' beds and a pram, and at least a dozen stuffed animals and dolls carried in by the demure-looking Alicia, all golden elf-locks and rose-petal complexion. Rosina chuckled. 'Just because I said she was a limb of Satan it doesn't mean she's not maternal. It goes with fighting other people's battles and a sort of mothering complex.'

Nat was a redhead, Tim dark and gipsy-like as was his mother. They were all great talkers, that was for sure, and it helped tremendously.

Zillah said as she tucked a battered-looking stuffed green frog against Alicia's pillow, 'Priscilla, this is too marvellous. Rosina tells me you're the daughter of this Seth Marchant she's always thought so much of. I'd not heard of you before, strangely enough, but I think you'll be right for our family. I felt so dreadful leaving them with anyone of Rosina's age, yet despite Barnabas being so anti, she's the only one I'd consider, as far as their happiness is concerned. I feel so torn between two loyalties. Rosina says you'll be here nights and weekends right through. I'll ring whenever I can, and promise me that if they're sick, or proving too much for Rosina, you'll send for me?'

'I promise. Oh, I think Keith's calling you. I'll keep them busy unpacking when you go off with Rosina. And Zillah, try to enjoy this adventure. It's a pity to spoil it by worrying over your family. Get all you can out of it. I daresay, like most parents, you're hardly ever off alone together. If Rosina and I can't manage this three, we ought to be able to. I've helped bring up my sister's children almost all their lives. She was widowed, but she doesn't need me any more —she's married again. I'll love this.'

'Oh, bless you . . . yes, Keith, I'm coming.'

Priscilla wasn't deceived by the children's matter-of-fact farewells to their parents. They knew perfectly well it was tougher on the older folk and she had an idea from something Nat muttered to them that he'd briefed them beforehand to play it cool. She asked them to show her round the property.

'No, I've always just dropped in on Rosina, never explored.'

Tim looked amazed. 'I couldn't stand that. I like to know all about people's houses and gardens.'

Priscilla nodded, 'So do I, as a rule, but somehow we never got round to it. Where does this path go?'

Alicia answered. 'Straight to the donkey-stables and paddocks.'

'Donkeys? Not really? How marvellous! I love them.'

What names those donkeys had— Jehosaphat, Ezekiel, Hannah. They were beige-coloured with darker patches on manes and tails and had velvety muzzles. The children laughed at Priscilla because she got so excited about them.

'I'll love riding these. I'm one of the ninnies who's scared of horses—it's being up high. But I reckon I'd manage on one of these. Would you teach me?'

They swaggered a bit and felt superior. Sure they could teach her. They pointed out another path that led over a little stream crossed by a rustic bridge. 'That leads to the chalet. Uncle Manuel built it ages ago to take their visitors because Aunt Rosina was always asking scads of people and cooking for them, and Uncle said they could have the chalet and jolly well cook for themselves. No good taking you over there yet because we're not allowed there by ourselves.' This was Nat.

Alicia said, 'And now Aunt says if somebody nice would take Jesmond Dene and let her live in the chalet, she'd have company on the property and less garden to look after. I'm always trying to think of two nice people who might get married and do that. Then we'd never have Aunt Rosina move away if she gets too old.'

Priscilla was surprised at the way she recoiled from the idea of anyone but Rosina ever living at Jesmond Dene.

It was quite a day, though enjoyable. At last the children were in bed, exhausted, and Rosina and Priscilla were relaxing in the dimness of the drawing-room, with breezes blowing in from the croquet lawn, and roses and lilies gleaming whitely from the herbaceous border beyond, like faintly-lit lanterns.

What a long companionable silence they had shared since sinking down in the big wing chairs. During it Priscilla had decided something. She'd resign from Lockhart's altogether and take this on for the three months. But she wouldn't tell her chief what she was doing or he'd try to persuade her to be here merely at nights and weekends. She just must cut away.

'Rosina, may I use your desk over there? I've some mail to get away.' She made several rough drafts, then wrote one out that satisfied her. She began,

'Dear Mr Lockhart,

'You heard something of my conversation with my brother-in-law the other day, so you may not be too surprised at this. He'd recommended a flat at the other end of Dunedin, but I feel I would be better to leave Dunedin altogether.

'I've enjoyed working at Lockhart's tremendously, so it will be quite a wrench, but a complete break is called for. I'll have a look round up here during my holiday. That will give you about ten days clear after receipt of this to look for someone else, but of course I'll return for about another week or so, to train my successor, if you wish this. I'm sure you'll find someone who'll appreciate the situation as much as I did. I loved the atmosphere of Lockhart's in both staff and management, something I'm sure which stemmed from your own policies.

'I won't worry about asking for a reference at this stage, but may have to call upon you for one if I see a position that would suit me.

'Trusting this isn't too disrupting for you,

'Yours sincerely,

'Priscilla Marchant.'

She had headed it care of her Christchurch friend, and would post the letter to her, asking her to mail it to Lockhart's box number. She wanted to make this break with her chief as complete as possible.

She got out her car, ran out the few miles to the airport, posted it there. He ought to get it not later than Tuesday. She wouldn't call round at the flat till tomorrow afternoon after church to pack her things and explain what she was doing—but not why—to Clarice. Clarice would be sulky, of course, and say it would mean she wouldn't get out with Roger so much at nights, but what odds? She'd sulked over more trifling things often enough.

CHAPTER THREE

THE transition to a different way of life was less painful than she'd expected, though perhaps it was merely that when the children were home there wasn't much time to miss the man who had coloured her working hours for her for months.

She fitted into life at Jesmond Dene as if she'd been a member of the family all her life. It was like a holiday when the children were at school and a bear-garden when they were home. But what fun they were, and so uninhibited. Not in the least introspective or reserved.

Alicia, Rosina vowed, had practically been a model child. Priscilla wouldn't have called her precisely that, finding tadpoles in the bathroom—not in the bath where Alicia had put them because she vowed their slimy-looking pond in the village was polluted; having her stuck up a tree where she'd climbed to put back some eggs she'd found on the ground beneath it, and quite unrepentant even when told it was last spring's infertile eggs and an old nest; and fishing her out of the rain-barrel because she'd mistaken a water-snail for a land-snail in danger of drowning.

Nat gashed his knee and had to spend a day at home, and Timothy had to be persuaded that though no doubt slugs had their uses, he was not to rescue them from the weed-bucket and tenderly deposit them back under Rosina's Sweet Williams. Dougal and Elspeth were a great help, dropping in to see how they were getting on, and Priscilla, though conscious that her own efforts in the writing line were small beer indeed, was delighted to find Elspeth was Elspeth Cameron, the novelist.

She knew a moment of wild regret when her chief's letter reached her. He said all the things any employer might, at

losing a valuable staff member, then was exceedingly sweet
on a personal note.

'Might I say, Priscilla, how much I admire you for
cutting loose like this from an intolerable situation? I
am aware it must have been very painful for you, but it
seems you haven't hesitated. Don't whip yourself over
it. I'm sure you've no cause to feel any real guilt. These
situations do occur and have to be faced and conquered,
and that, I'm sure, you have done.

'I'm quite often in Christchurch where I'm sure you'll
find a good position. To facilitate that, here is your
reference, though you may not need it yet, as you're
seeking a job while still in employment. But it may give
you that extra pull that's needed. I'd like very much to
keep in touch. When you're settled, would you send me
your address? I take it that the one you wrote from
was a friend's? Even if you go further afield I'd like to
know where you are.

'As I said earlier in this letter, we'll miss you horribly
in a business way. The organisation will be poorer for
your resignation.

'Yours,

'Peter B. Lockhart.'

Priscilla saw it through a haze of tears. It was hand-
written; he hadn't dictated it. The reference was superb.
Priscilla didn't sleep very well that night.

Rosina was extremely incurious about Priscilla's job, merely
thought of it as a run-of-the-mill office one, and when she
was told that Priscilla wanted to get away from the family
set-up and a little about it, she very much approved.

Rosina was aware that Priscilla was dropping in salary
but didn't dream how much. So Priscilla kept it vague,
knowing that if she mentioned the leading firm of drapers
in Dunedin, and that she'd been secretary to the owner,

Rosina would guess it was exceedingly well paid. 'I'll let my flat, Rosina, and the rent from that will certainly make up for loss of salary. I've thought for long enough I was tired of being tied to an office desk.'

Rosina had chuckled. 'Don't expect your nice brother-in-law to approve. He'll think you've left off one yoke to assume another. But I'm not going to be a hypocrite and pretend I'm not thinking of you as a godsend. You are the answer to all Barnabas objected to. I'm going to enjoy seeing his face when he knows I've got help.'

On the Friday Priscilla noticed Rosina was limping and trying to conceal it. She tackled her.

Rosina said defensively, 'Well, I don't suppose it's serious —a sort of burning sensation at the back of my knee. I can't see it in the mirror. It'll probably be gone in a day or two.'

'Not if you keep walking on it. Up on that couch with you.'

She whistled as it came into view. An enormous spreading dark stain like a concentrated bruise was situated right on the bend. 'I'd think a varicose vein has burst, Rosina. Not anything to worry over provided you're sensible, but it means keeping right off it.'

Rosina looked horrified. 'Oh, surely not? I can't possibly be laid aside just now when Barnabas is nearly due. What would he say?'

'To the devil with Barnabas! He couldn't say more than: "I told you so." And that won't break any bones. Besides, when he finds me here, young, strong, healthy, what can he say? Believe me, I'm more than a match for Barnabas.' She sketched some shadow boxing.

Rosina giggled. 'I believe you are. But he will create, I know it. And I will not have the children made to feel nuisances.'

'Now look, Rosina, it could have been awkward had you been on your own, but when he knows I'm here for the entire length the Darfields are in Papua, he can't say a thing. What a blessing I gave up my job!'

Rosina promptly burst into tears. This all added up to the idea of the horrible Barnabas as a positive monster. Yes, for sure he'd be pompous, portly, prosperous.

Rosina mopped up. 'They're tears of happiness and relief, dear child. Remembering I'm not on my own.'

'You'd better ring the wretched man and get it over with. He gave you a week and it's almost up. Better to tell him you've got someone than have him come out here and finding you on the couch. I'll phone Doctor Mark and you can phone your nephew later, the ogre.'

The doctor decreed two weeks' rest and little activity for a bit longer, said, 'Grand thing you've got Miss Marchant. Couldn't be better.' Priscilla hoped Barnabas felt the same.

She heard Rosina using the phone beside her bed but didn't eavesdrop. Rosina would make her sound like a ministering angel. Heaven send the beastly Barnabas didn't hot-foot it out late this afternoon and arrive when the children were in the middle of a ding-dong battle, and the place a shambles.

Rosina called her. She didn't look in the least squashed. 'He's coming out right away to look you over. What he said when he knew I'd had the children almost a week was unprintable. "Who is this girl?" he thundered. "Some flibbertygibbet as mad as yourself?" I said, "Dear me no, this is the daughter of an old friend. I haven't seen her for some time and she happened to call in and as she's free, offered to stay for the entire three months. Very used to children," I said, "and is a good disciplinarian. Added to that, the children just love her." I think he thinks you're in the forty bracket. You wouldn't like to powder your hair a little at the temples, would you, to add to that impression?'

'Rosina! You're incorrigible. I can almost find it in me to be sorry for your nephew. Still, I'm sure I can convince him I can manage this household. The main thing will be to convince him I can manage *you*. So you can look a little nervous of me as you would if you were under the thumb of a very severe nurse. Now I'll pick some flowers for that

vase—those look a little wilted. Good job your room is
downstairs, but so you won't feel too much out of it, when
beastly Barnabas has departed I'll fix you up a day-bed in
the drawing-room. But not a word about that. I want him
to regard you as not daring to put a foot out of bed. Could
we invent a former nursing career for me, do you think?'

Rosina was popped into night-clothes, arranged against a
bank of pale pink pillows, a pile of magazines and some
fruit put within reach. Priscilla made a dainty afternoon
tea, putting out the silver tea-service on a basket table,
sandwiches with cool green slices of cucumber and lettuce,
dotted with parsley sprigs; wedges of a cherry-cake she'd
made that morning, ginger gems spread with butter, the
best china.

Rosina giggled. 'How this will impress him! Though I
wish you'd looked a little older. You look a dream in that
butter-coloured dress with the nut-brown epaulettes. It's
cool yet delectable.'

As Priscilla went out to pick the flowers she laughed back
over her shoulder. 'Good job I'm not afraid of Barnabas eating me. You make me sound positively edible!'

She decided on something fragrant . . . cottage roses in
palest pink, a few sprays of golden-throated honeysuckle,
purple verbena. She was mounting the curved steps when
she heard the car and paused.

The moment was upon her for meeting the horrible
Barnabas. Well before the children would arrive too. Good.
She felt cool, elegant, poised.

A Jag slid round the curve of the drive, looking as if it had
just been delivered from a sales showroom. He *would* own
a car like that, of course. It came to a perfect stop in front
of the steps. Priscilla, poised on the second one, turned,
smiling.

A man, not portly, slid from behind the wheel, got out,
advanced towards her, and took two quick steps. Then he
froze. So did Priscilla. Her smile became a grimace.

Here was a turn-up for the book! It wasn't the horrible

Barnabas, but how passionately she wished it was. It was quite beyond belief, but here was Mr Lockhart! How had he found out where she was? Had he gone to her flat for something? Perhaps asked Clarice for her Christchurch address? What would he think?

But it was at that moment she realised that he too was in a state of shock, that he'd not expected to find her here. He was staring at her as if he couldn't believe his eyes.

As one they both moved. Priscilla brought her right foot down from the step to join the other. Mr Lockhart began walking towards her again. Then when he was nearer she could see the veins in his throat standing out in anger and he stopped again and said between his teeth, 'I have a feeling I've missed my cue somehow. What the hell are *you* doing in my aunt's house?

Priscilla had a feeling of the world of trees and blooms swinging up towards the sky and of her eyes swivelling rapidly to keep pace with the movement.

She said stupidly, 'Your *aunt's* house? That's just not possible. *You're* not the horrible Barnabas!'

His lips tightened. 'I am. Peter Barnabas Lockhart, and the adjective is a playful one, not meant to be taken seriously. But why did you make out to me, your boss, that you were in Christchurch?'

There just wasn't any answer to that.

Priscilla's brain went on repeating that over and over to her. *There just isn't a answer to that.* But Peter Barnabas Lockhart had other ideas. He said in a staccato tone, 'I'm waiting for an answer, Miss Marchant. What the hell are you doing here? And why did you lead me to believe you were in Christchurch?'

Priscilla had always prided herself on being a yes-no, black-and-white sort of person, but here was no clear-cut answer. She felt the colour leaving her face and had a moment of desperate hoping that she'd not faint. That would be the final humiliation.

With a superhuman effort she steadied herself. 'I—I—

thought it best—for a variety of reasons—to make it look as if—as if I'd made a complete break. I——'

'Then if you have a variety of reasons, how about giving me one of them? Only one, that's all I ask.'

If only her brain didn't feel so paralysed, so incapable of summoning up something that would sound even faintly feasible. But what *could* sound feasible? How could she say, 'I wanted to make a complete break from my job because I've fallen in love with you?'

Her mouth was so dry she had to try to swallow. It wasn't very successful. She'd never before realised that eyes could look as chilly as the ice-blue of a crevasse. She finally managed to say feebly, 'My reasons are completely private to myself. That's all I can offer in the way of explanation.'

His lips were a thin line. 'That's no explanation at all. Merely underlining the fact that you lied to me. You must have sent that letter to a friend in Christchurch to mail back to me. Why?'

'I've told you, I can't tell you why.'

'Does this friend know why?'

'No. I merely said I'd a personal reason for letting my former boss think I was working up north. She's a close friend, not curious. Not young. She knows how to keep her own counsel.'

'For which many thanks, Miss Marchant, otherwise what would she have spread around? That as a boss I'm a womaniser, a persistent one. I can't think of any other reason that would occur to an outsider. Weren't you afraid she'd think you devious?'

'No. She would trust me to have a good reason.'

'How very odd. I thought I could trust you, but just when I seemed to be getting to know my very reserved secretary a little better, and liking what I found, I've come to the conclusion that I can't trust her at all.'

Priscilla bit her lip and to her chagrin thought tears were going to overwhelm her. The horrible Barnabas noticed it. He held up his hand. 'Please, not tears. That's supposed

to be the weapon men can't fight, but it would have no
effect on me.'

She suddenly felt rage possess her and was glad. It was
better than feeling guilty because she'd deceived him, and
scared because she dared not let him guess at her feelings
for him. She said hotly, 'I can well believe that. You've probably had much experience with tears ... with the spoiled
and pampered Melisande. I've seen her pout time and
again when you've refused her something.'

He was infuriatingly nonchalant about that. 'Exactly. But
at least Melisande is transparent. Tell me one thing. Are you
keeping your whereabouts secret from everyone? For instance, does your brother-in-law know where you are?'

She stared. 'Yes, of course.' She felt, as his expression
hardened, that he disliked her more than ever now. Why?

'And your sister?'

She made a helpless gesture, bewildered. 'Again of course.
Clarice is sending on my mail. She thinks I'm slightly mad
giving up a well-paid position for this, and I'm sure she
thinks my irrational behaviour is due to my being a
spinster.' She managed a flicker of amusement. This time
he positively scowled.

She went on hurriedly, 'Look, you heard what went on
between me and my brother-in-law. His marriage stands a
better chance with me out of it, but surely you didn't
imagine I'd cut myself off from them. I *had* intended to
look for a position in Christchurch, but when I found Rosina
in need of help with three children, and that it would give
their mother greater peace of mind to know a younger
person was sharing the responsibility, I felt this was ideal.
It would give me a breathing-space too. It seems incredible
now, in face of your disapproval, but I actually thought
I'd been led here. I happen to believe in those things. I
thought I was meant to be here at this particular time, at
a crossroads in my own life, and when Rosina was in need.'

His lip curled. 'I'm not one who gives much credence to
this smug talk of being led. I'm inclined to think people

bend circumstances to their own particular desires, and then talk glibly of their being led ... when all the time they're going their own selfish way. What happened to you was that your courage failed you—you couldn't quite pull up the anchor and launch out into the deep. I'm extremely disappointed in you. Till tonight I was admiring you for putting a distance between yourself and—well, the situation. I thought Roger had a real problem, a far greater problem than yours, and the further away you would be, the better for him.'

Priscilla said through stiff lips, 'I find these strictures an intrusion on my private affairs. They're nothing to do with you. I'm out here on the Taieri, perhaps twenty miles from Roger and Clarice. After all, his idea was for me to take a flat in another suburb, I was the one who thought I'd go further. But things changed. I came here.'

His face altered. 'Yes, you came here. Why? How did it all come about? And why did my aunt not tell me your name? Did you involve her in your deception too? Your quite inexplicable deception! Though for how long you thought to keep it up, I don't know.' He stopped, clutched his head, said, 'Look, for goodness' sake put me in the picture. I'm all at sea. You can't have told Rosina you worked for me, because you didn't know I was her nephew. Must be because she never calls me anything but Barnabas. But didn't she ask where you'd worked formerly?'

'I think you'd better stop firing questions at me. I can't sort them out. I'm just as confused myself. You started it anyway. I thought I was just delivering Horticultural Society notices. How could I have guessed that one letter was to an aunt of yours?'

'Granted. I'd followed up my ultimatum of a day or two earlier—that I'd see Zillah myself if she persisted in this —with one or two other reasons why she ought not to assume this responsibility. I thought you could deliver it with the others.'

'Well, I sat down on the seat outside the fence. It was a

tranquil spot and I wanted to sort myself out from my turmoil of thoughts.'

'I can understand that.'

'How good of you. It makes you almost human, Barnabas.'

'Why don't you make it what you're thinking and call me *horrible* Barnabas?'

'Well, if you know what I'm thinking, you can add that very apt adjective yourself,' she retorted.

'I ought to laugh, this is so childish, but I want you to get on telling me the why and wherefore of it before my darling aunt comes out to ask when I'm coming inside.'

'Oh, she can't. Didn't she tell you on the phone?'

'Can't what? Tell me what?'

'Can't come outside. She burst a varicose vein. It has to have complete rest. Now aren't you glad I'm here?'

'I *knew* something like this would happen! Aunt Rosina will not realise her age. Running round after three imps of Satan ... it's plain ridiculous. Something like this was bound to happen.'

'It wasn't the children's fault at all. It happened before they got here. If it's anybody's fault, it's yours.'

His jaw dropped. 'My fault! You must be raving mad! You——'

'It was your fault she climbed the Wellingtonia and got treed. If you hadn't said you wouldn't put it past her to go climbing with the children, she'd never have even thought of attempting it ... so she thought she'd prove she could, before they got here, just to show you. That was where I came in.'

'Where you came in?'

'Yes. I was sitting on the seat when I heard her sw—— when I heard her call out.'

'When you heard her swearing. I know my aunt.' For the first time she saw a faint softening of his expression.

'So I rushed in and she kept calling out to guide me. And there she was, dangling.'

'Dangling? I thought you meant she'd fallen down, or got stuck.'

'No, she'd have got down as easily as she got up, had not the hem of her frock caught on a branch above her. I edged up past her and got it off, that's all. And Dougal thought she ought not to stay by herself in case she'd suffered any damage not apparent at the time.'

'You mean like scratches? Because getting hooked up couldn't cause harm.'

'Oh, we both fell out of the tree when we'd almost got to the bottom. Fortunately Rosina fell on top of me. Dougal hauled us up and took us into the house.'

'Dougal MacNab? Why didn't he go up after her if he was here? My word, that's fast going! To be on Christian name terms with the parish minister already.'

Priscilla glared at him. 'I call his wife by her first name too. I was asked to—they're that sort of people. You once accused me of being too formal about names. Now——'

'So I did. Seems incredible now. But——'

'And Dougal only arrived as we fell out of the tree.'

'Anyway,' he went on, 'none of this really explains why you've given up a top position and taken on something that can't carry much pay. Sounds to me as if you snatched at anything that meant you'd be a little distance away, but not out of reach!'

His face held an accusing look. It was beyond her. It seemed as if he thought she was the possessive type, that she hadn't wanted Clarice to re-marry. That she'd agreed with Roger, when he'd tackled her, then had regrets about really making a new life for herself. It made her furious, thinking of all the times she'd longed to live her own life. Then she steadied herself. At least this meant he hadn't guessed her real reason for leaving Lockhart's. That was the one thing he mustn't know. How intensely humiliating it would be for him to know she cared for him so much she couldn't go on working for him! Embarrassing for him too. Especially when she was working for his aunt.

Her eyes met his more frankly. 'Not everybody looks for the highest paid job. Happiness is much more important. Or if not happiness, less strain, less feeling of being caught up in a treadmill. There's a lot of pressure in big business.'

His expression changed again but was still unreadable. 'That makes Lockhart's sound like a rat-race. All business is competitive, of course, yet neither my father nor myself are in it solely for profit. We could have sold it long ago, and had just as much income out of investing our capital, and a lot less worry, but the firm would have been swallowed up in one of the big chains, and a lot of redundancy would have occurred. Even if some may feel caught up in a treadmill, almost all of them need their wages and some actually enjoy it.'

Priscilla felt as if she'd been guilty of accusing him of capitalism, which was absurd, but she flushed, said, 'I didn't mean the way you Lockharts conduct your business, because it's the best I've seen. Perhaps I meant I didn't want to stay in a secretarial position for ever. I'm grateful I've always had a highly-paid job. I needed a good salary when my father died comparatively early in life, and my sister was widowed too. But now, at last, I feel I might be able to live my own life and do my own thing.'

His attention was caught by that, deflecting his anger. 'Your own thing? Which is?'

'In my case, a hobby which could prove to be more than that. I write—articles, short stories, occasional verse, for magazines. Like most writers I dream of someday finding time to write a book. If I take on a less exacting job for a time—in this case three months—I may find a few hours now and then when my brain is fresh. Before my sister married again, my free hours were largely taken up mowing lawns and gardening. Now, does that satisfy you why I've taken on a job that in the eyes of some would be definitely down-grading?'

His lip curled. Sarcasm or wryness? But why would it be wryness? 'It satisfies my curiosity as to why you've taken it, but not as to why you had to deceive me over it.'

'Well, there's nothing I can do about that. I told you my reasons were private. I don't want to keep discussing it— it's nothing to do with you. You're simply my former boss.'

'Thank you. I've always looked on my employees—most of them—as friends too. This not only disgusts me, it hurts. I prided myself on being a good judge of character.'

'In that case, Mr Lockhart, would you like me to return you that reference? I remember it spoke of my absolute integrity. You might like to modify it, couch it in less glowing terms?'

'That's so ridiculous and petty it hardly needs an answer. I wrote that reference as I knew you then, as you appeared to me in business life. The fact that we're now involved personally doesn't affect that.'

'We're hardly involved with each other. You've spoken your mind. Let it rest there.'

'Of course we're involved. You're looking after my father's sister, for whom, in a very real way while Mum and Dad are overseas, I'm responsible.' He paused, said, 'She's bound to ask you some day where you worked. I know she's vague and other-worldly, but some day it will occur to her. I think we'd better tell her right away that you used to work for me. Let me see . . . she's bound to wonder why I didn't know, if you told her you wrote from here resigning your former position. Oh, I know, we'll tell her you put your Dunedin address on it and didn't mention your new job in case I tried to persuade you to give me part-time.'

Priscilla curled her lip then. 'You were scathing when I pretended I was in Christchurch, yet it appears you aren't above bending the truth to suit yourself. How self-righteous of you!'

She didn't like the look he gave her. She wasn't meant to like it. 'It's rather different. My aunt sounded delighted with her new companion. The daughter of her former solicitor, she said. I don't want to upset her. Although I was against her taking on the Darfield children, now they're here, and their parents already in Papua, she sure needs that help. She may be slightly perturbed to think that through her I lost an efficient secretary, but we can't conceal the whole thing. But we can water it down. Anyway, Melisande would give us away.'

'Melisande?'

'Naturally, she comes out here with me at times.'

Of course. The scatty girl-friend of Rosina's nephew! She said, 'Then ... as we seem to have reached some sort of compromise, I suggest we go in. She'll wonder what on earth is keeping you from going in to see her. We can play down the fact that the surprise of seeing each other made for a confrontation. We can simply say we yarned about the long arm of coincidence.'

'That will do very nicely, Miss Marchant. I value my aunt's peace of mind.'

'Do you? I rather thought you'd been her main worry—in fact dread—this last little while.'

'My concern was for her welfare. To see she isn't imposed upon. It happens to her all the time. Now, let's pull ourselves together. She can read me like a book. Fortunately, with your colouring, you don't show the signs of anger. You look as cool as a cucumber.'

Then he stared, because Priscilla laughed. He said stiffly, 'I'm supposed to have a ready sense of humour, but I fail to see anything funny at all in that.'

'You couldn't be expected to. My sense of humour trips me up at times too. It was something your aunt said earlier, a triviality. Let's go in.'

Rosina was sitting up in bed looking absurdly like a child anticipating a treat, not one expecting a censorious nephew. 'Hullo, dear boy, how nice to see you.'

'Is it?' He bent to kiss her. 'Rosina, you'll never go to heaven when you die. I have it on Miss Marchant's authority that you've been positively dreading my coming.'

She gave him a frank look. 'Oh, I *would* have dreaded it if I hadn't got my own way *first*. But not now. The children are here and I've been incredibly lucky in having Miss Marchant arrive on my doorstep at the very time I most needed her, and free to take on a job like this.'

'Free indeed!' he muttered, but Rosina was sweeping on.

'You've taken so long to come in, I realise you must have got well acquainted by now, and you'll have no doubts either as to her suitability.'

He said dryly, though smiling as if indeed it was a joke on himself, 'I know better than you dream, Aunt, how efficient she is. All unknown to you, you've pinched my secretary. You could have knocked me down with a feather when I got out of my car to find my Miss Marchant tripping down the steps. It all adds up to this wish of my grandfather's that there'd always be a Peter Lockhart at the head of the firm, and the fact that in the family circle I'm always Barnabas. I knew she was on holiday, then had a letter from her saying she wished to terminate her position with us, but didn't imagine that you, of all people, had done the pirating.'

Rosina, who normally had the greatest knack of taking the unusual with nonchalance, looked completely shocked for once. She fell back on her pillows. 'My dear boy! This can't be true! Oh dear, have I upset you very much? But how——?'

Priscilla had to admire his acting. 'Now, no twittering. It's most amusing. You see, naturally Miss Marchant put her Dunedin address on her letter, and gave me notice, offering to return to put her successor through her paces should I want that, and didn't mention she'd already found herself a little niche, even if it's just a temporary one.'

Priscilla helped it along. 'If only I'd said to you where I'd worked, Rosina—or if you'd asked.'

Rosina, recovering, looked mischievous. 'I'm glad you didn't. I'd never have had the nerve to filch his secretary from him. He was cross enough with me as it was, and if he'd thought it was going to mean disruption in his office, his fury would have known no bounds.'

Barnabas waved a despairing hand, said to Priscilla, 'See what I mean? She sounds terrified and goes her own sweet way regardless.' To his aunt he said mock-severely, 'She honestly thought I was detestable ... as your unknown nephew. She said: "But *you* can't be the horrible Barnabas!" Really, Aunt, you're ruining my reputation.'

'But no one who knew you would think you horrible, Barnabas, and if Miss Marchant has worked for you she'll know how sweet you are.'

'*Sweet?*' Barnabas looked even more outraged. 'Aunt, no employee ever thinks her employer is sweet. Now what about this leg of yours? Has Mark Gainsborough seen it? How bad——'

She held up a hand. 'Nothing to flap about, dear boy. Rest will do it and Priscilla is a born nurse. I'm taking full advantage of the chance to lie in bed and read.'

He said slowly, 'It'll be all right till you begin to get bored. I know you of old. The moment the doctor says you can be up for an hour, you'll make it three and dash into the garden.'

'She won't,' said Priscilla. 'I'm here. I promise you that.'

'She'll do it when your back is turned, and with those three here your back will be turned pretty often. They may have been angels of light so far ... I guess Zillah would impress it on them to start with, but you can't know what's in store for you.'

'She does, Barnabas. I put her in the picture before they arrived. They've already lived up to their reputation and she can cope with it all, doesn't get upset.'

He looked uneasy. 'Meaning she lets them go their own way? Their wild, unpredictable way? They need——'

Rosina broke in. 'They need a firm hand ... and that's what they're getting. Priscilla discovered last night that Nat had skipped his homework. He said airily that he intended getting up early in the morning to do it. She made him do it while one of the underwater features was on T.V. —his favourite. He muttered that she was as bad as his

mother, but he did it, and did it well. From now on, he's
going to make sure it's done before they start watching.

'As for Alicia ... she was obviously trading on the fact
that Priscilla was strange, therefore wouldn't like to discipline her. She found out how wrong she was mighty soon.
"I'm standing in for your mother," quoth Priscilla, "therefore I'll do exactly what she would do under these circumstances ... spank you." And spank her she did ... on the
bottom where the Good Lord meant children to be spanked
... then explained that she hoped to deliver all three of
them back to their mother with no broken limbs or skulls
and that she always spanked for dangerous practices and
direct disobedience. Alicia has walked warily since. Then
Priscilla added that she spanked for lying too.'

Priscilla found Barnabas's eye fixed firmly on her. Sar-
donic, that was the expression. Not hard to read this time.
She found her colour rising. Rosina said kindly, 'Don't blush
because I'm praising you, dear. This is to set his mind at
rest that you're the right person in the right place at the
right time.'

Priscilla said hastily, 'I'll go and make the tea.'

She thought of all the times she'd poured his office tea.
It gave her a feeling of unreality. Was this true, or a dream?
She was sitting in Mr Peter B. Lockhart's aunt's bedroom,
and now she could only think of him as Barnabas. She was
a housekeeper, not a secretary, and whereas once she'd been
a trusted employee now he thought of her as a liar.

She hoped he'd depart before the children came home
from school, because youngsters always knew when they
were not wanted. Well, that might mean, if he so disliked
children, that he wouldn't come out here so much when
they were staying, with or without Melisande. Just imagine,
if Melisande had ever called him anything but darling, she
might have known he was Barnabas!

Rosina sensed nothing amiss. She even said, with an air
of concession, 'When I'm on my feet again, dear boy, if you
wanted Priscilla in for a few mornings to help you get

things straight, I'd be willing to spare her.'

'Good of you, but once an employee has given notice, I think it's best for them to quit. It's never a satisfactory period.'

Rosina was shocked. 'With some employees perhaps, but never would it be like that with Priscilla. She's the soul of integrity, wouldn't slack off.'

His voice was hatefully suave. 'I'm sure she's the soul of integrity. She wouldn't turn a hair. Look at her now. Who'd think it was a shock to meet the nephew of her new employer and find him her former boss? Cool as a cucumber as always.'

Rosina burst out laughing, turned to Priscilla, said, 'You see .. it comes natural to compare you to food.'

Priscilla chuckled. Barnabas glared at them. 'Do I get told what's so funny about that? Or told again my sense of humour's at fault?'

Priscilla said, 'Oh, I didn't say that, just that it was a triviality and you couldn't be expected to understand.'

He cocked an eyebrow at his aunt. She said, 'I told her she looked a dream in that butter-coloured dress with the nutbrown epaulettes ... cool and delectable. Don't you think she looks good enough to eat, Barnabas?'

'She does. But then cucumber always gives me indigestion.'

Rosina looked surprised, but went on, 'I was naughty, wasn't I, Barnabas, on the phone? I made her sound in the sere and yellow. I did suggest she might powder her hair at the temples, to make it look greying. Just as well she didn't. You'd have been furious, to think your one-time secretary played a trick on you like that. Oh dear, I've just thought, Priscilla. If you were Barnabas's secretary, you're giving up a fabulous wage for a token remuneration. Why on earth did you do it?'

Oddly, it was Barnabas who saved her. He said, quite quickly, 'Didn't you know she writes? Short stories, articles, poems, all are grist to her mill. She has an ambition to write a novel—well, a book, she said. Her job at Lockharts didn't give her enough time. She'd been thinking of taking a part-time one for long enough, something that would give her more time at her desk. So this, for three months, could have been ideal. When you're on your feet again, she must have an hour or two each day, on writing.'

Rosina looked dismayed. 'My dear Priscilla, how frustrating for you that this should have happened! But it may heal more quickly than the doctor thinks, then you must get some time in the mornings to yourself.'

Priscilla said quickly, 'It doesn't matter. Mr Lockhart, you oughtn't to have said anything. I've all my life in front of me to find my niche. This three months can be an interim period. I'll plan some serious writing while I'm here and tackle it when I leave. It's not a novel, by the way, it's a book for children, so think what copy these three are giving me. I had an idea the other day, shopping in the village. I might sell my unit in town and buy one of those pioneer cottages in the main street and do it up to use as a writing retreat. I might even find a part-time job in one of the shops when I leave here.' She stopped, said to Rosina, 'What is it? You look as if someone's just handed you the moon.'

Barnabas groaned. 'Rosina, watch it! Miss Marchant doesn't know you as I do. I distrust that look. It matches the one of Alicia's that we dread. Her crusading look ... and it always involves us in something.'

Rosina's hazel eyes widened in innocence. 'How can you say such a thing? I'm no nine-year-old, I'm past three-score-and-ten and very sensible. It involves *you* in nothing.'

'If it involves you, it concerns me.'

She waved that aside. 'Not this. Priscilla can have the Thistledown House. For writing in, I mean. Manuel's study would be ideal for her. She may not get much done while we have the children, but afterwards it would be perfect, a solution to all our problems. Then you'd never have to worry about me again.'

Barnabas looked more apprehensive than a man relieved of a burden. Priscilla said, 'Thistledown House? Some place you own in the village?'

Rosina said, 'It's the chalet. I've not had time to take you over it yet. Manuel built it for us to retire to when we got too old to manage this big house and garden, but he died in his full health and strength, bless him, at sixty-eight, so age never wearied him. What we'd thought would be ideal was for Barnabas to marry and bring his bride here to Jesmond Dene, but it's hardly likely to happen now.'

Barnabas said, 'What do you mean? I'm not a confirmed bachelor at thirty-two!'

'No, but you seem to be making a fool of yourself over Melisande again, and you can't see her here in this set-up, can you?'

Priscilla felt decidedly *de trop*. Rosina was carrying frankness too far. Barnabas burst out laughing, 'Look at Miss Marchant's face! You've really shocked her. She's wishing herself elsewhere.'

'I certainly am,' said Priscilla fervently. 'I just wish the children would arrive. Oh, it sounds as if they're coming—listen to those cycle bells. Mr Lockhart, there's just one thing. So far I'm managing them fine. They're high-spirited, naughty at times, sweet at others, but biddable. They aren't playing on our sympathy because their parents aren't here, mainly because Rosina makes them feel loved and wanted. I don't want them to feel nuisances. If you can't put up with having them round, it would be kinder to cut your visit short. There! You seem to be a candid family. I hope you're fair enough to put up with equal candour from me, for the children's sakes.'

CHAPTER FOUR

How disconcerting it was therefore for Priscilla the next moment. The children burst in, with even more than their accustomed delight at getting home, and all three hurled themselves upon Barnabas.

He'd risen to meet them, arms flung wide. Alicia leapt clean up into his arms. 'Uncle Barney, we saw your new car. Nat said only you would have one like that.' She bestowed a rapturous kiss on him and even the fact that she had a gnawed-down candy-stick in her hand didn't seem to diminish his obvious pleasure in seeing them. The boys contented themselves with a hug, and Tim said, 'The car's a beaut. Can we get in it?'

'For sure. I'll come out with you in a jiffy. Alicia, have you a hanky? Would you mind wiping my left ear? Otherwise I'll stick to my pillow tonight.'

She looked shocked. 'Don't you wash your face before you go to bed?'

'Yes, but if I'm not showering, I'm afraid I skip my ears, they're so fiddly. But I'm very thorough with them in the mornings. Miss Marchant would tell you that.'

This reduced the three of them to momentary silence, then, 'Miss Marchant? Priscilla? But she doesn't live with you.'

Barnabas's blue eyes were dancing as they met Priscilla's brown ones above Alicia's flaxen head. 'No, but she used to be my secretary, and all secretaries get a good view of their boss's ears when he's dictating to them.'

Timothy came straight to the point. He fixed his dark eyes on Priscilla. 'Why didn't you tell us you used to work for him?'

She played safe and said vaguely, 'I always called my

61

boss Mr Lockhart and some of the older members of staff made it Mr Peter. So I'd no idea your Uncle Barney was my old chief. I suppose you aren't real relations anyway, are you? So what with Claremonts and Darfields I couldn't realise.'

Barnabas came in swiftly, 'Not related by blood but by other ties. Not kin, but kith. And sometimes kith means more than kin.'

Priscilla felt rebuked. She said lamely, 'Well, I mean nobody mentioned a Lockhart.'

Alicia said, 'I like that word. Kith. That means I'm kith to you, does it, Uncle Barnabas?'

He nodded. 'You're very kith to me. Hullo, who's that in the doorway?' It was another little girl of Alicia's age.

'It's my new friend, Nerolie Palmerston. They've just come to Fair-acre, so she's a bit lonely. Come on in, Nerolie. This is Aunt Rosina and Uncle Barney and Priscilla who's helping Aunt cope with us. Could she be kith to us too, Uncle Barney?'

'She could. Hullo, Nerolie, come in. Where did you live before?'

She ventured in. She had a pixie face, with dark eyes, was rather intense-looking, and had softly waving dark hair clustered about a creamy forehead. She would become a beauty.

Her voice was pleasing too, though it had an odd maturity. 'We lived in Christchurch. My father is the new Postmaster here. Alicia said it would be all right for me to come home with her.'

Rosina said warmly, 'Of course it is. Alicia and the boys can bring anyone home they want to.'

Alicia said anxiously, 'Can she have a really big afternoon tea? I know we're only allowed two pieces, but she's hungry. She didn't have a very big lunch.'

Priscilla saw Barnabas glance quickly at Nerolie. She thought he suppressed a grin. Rosina said, 'I think we can relax that rule today for you all, seeing you're entertaining.

But eat now and don't keep nibbling up till dinnertime, because Priscilla has a very nice meal prepared for you.'

Alicia seized the opportunity. 'Could Nerolie stay for it to, it would be such a nice change for her.'

Barnabas said swiftly, 'Not tonight. You see, Aunt Rosina has hurt her leg and has to be waited on, and it makes extra for Miss Marchant. When your aunt is up and about again, you can bring friends in for tea.'

Priscilla opened her mouth to say it wouldn't be any trouble, then closed it again as Barnabas shook his head at her. She mustn't antagonise him any more. She said instead, 'Come on out to the kitchen and you can sit up at the table there for your snack, then go out into the garden to play.'

When she came back Barnabas said, 'Glad you caught on. Nerolie is probably going to be one of Alicia's lame dogs. She has all the signs—the pathetic air, the diffidence.'

'What can you mean? It's good a child isn't too forward the first time in a strange house, and she's too beautifully dressed to be neglected.'

'You'll find out. Alicia is so firmly attached to lost causes and championing those who are wronged, she really inspires other children to play on it. I dimly suspect that if Nerolie started off with a small lunch, she also had most of Alicia's.'

Priscilla said shortly, 'I think you've got an over-active imagination, Mr Lockhart. I'm quite capable of sorting out this for myself. I was a member of a family of three, and I practically reared my sister's boy and girl.'

'How did your sister take that?'

Priscilla's brows came down, 'Mr Lockhart ... that sounds disapproving. In no way did I wish to take their mother's place, but when Clarice was widowed, there were things I took on in the children's father's place.'

He nodded. 'It's not always wise. You provide the prop so the clinging vine continues to cling. That's the trouble with Alicia. She fights other people's battles so they lose the power to stand up for themselves. I think they should be left to develop their own potential. The contrast can be cruel. They look even weaker against a strong personality. So don't encourage Alicia.'

Rosina stared at her nephew. 'I've never heard you go on like this before. Barnabas, you're being horrible!'

Priscilla went wicked. 'He certainly is, but when in my shock at meeting my boss, I said, "But *you* can't be the horrible Barnabas," he told me the adjective was a playful one, not meant to be taken seriously. Now I'm beginning to wonder.'

Rosina said severely, 'And if he doesn't stop criticising my godsend, I'll begin to wonder myself. Barnabas, you were talking of a family and situation you know nothing about, and the criticism is implied. I want to hear no more of it. *I'm* leaning on Priscilla at the moment, but it doesn't mean I'll be doing it indefinitely, yet normally, people lean on *me*. It's all a matter of tides.'

'Tides? My dear aunt, you're like a grasshopper . . . what do you mean?'

'At certain times everything seems at an ebb in our lives. That's when we need help. No doubt Priscilla's sister did for a time. Now she's married again, Priscilla's too sensible to keep it up. Barnabas, do take her over the Thistledown House while the children are eating and show her Manuel's study. Nothing could be more opportune. Off with you!'

Barnabas bowed to his aunt. 'I obey you. I hope you chalk up a good mark for me—I must get back into grace again. Miss Marchant, may I escort you to your place of future inspiration?'

'Very well . . . but not too long. I don't want the children to tire your aunt.'

They went through the playroom, took the path through what the children called the Mini-copse, a place of woodland beauty, bird-calls and the song of a brook. They crossed over the tiny humpy-backed bridge—a place of harmony, not antagonism.

Priscilla said, 'I'm sorry you've had your time taken up like this, Mr Lockhart, especially on late shopping night. I'll take a quick look over, then you can go.'

His mouth twitched. 'How dismissing! Our roles seem to have changed. It's just not done to dismiss either royalty or one's boss. Oh, don't tell me I'm no longer your boss. I'll come and go as I please here. In any case, I'm taking tonight off. I'm staying for tea—Rosina asked me.'

She said, 'So your seeming solicitude for me in the matter of Nerolie not staying merely means you felt you couldn't stand four children!'

He burst out laughing. 'Come, Miss Marchant, you saw the welcome the kids gave me. I'll never forget your face. Be fair. I still think you don't realise that given an inch, Alicia will fill my aunt's house with an 'ell of a lot of waifs and strays. I say, you're supposed to laugh ... that was quite a good pun. Give your sense of humour an airing.'

She tried to look disdainful and failed. Laughter just bubbled up in her. She clung to the railing. 'Oh dear, I'm being absurd. I feel about nine years old again, having a spat with Andrew. All meaningless too.'

'What do you mean by that?'

She answered without thinking. 'No real feeling behind any of the quarrelling. That's how it is with kids.'

'Exactly. And no real enmity between us, which is as it should be.'

Priscilla suddenly felt uneasy. She'd left his employ because she was afraid of revealing her feelings for him. Now they seemed in even more intimate involvement. She mustn't be too friendly. So she said, 'It was rather different. Andrew and I were brother and sister, we trusted each other. But I deceived you. You said you don't trust me any longer. For Rosina's peace of mind we must be friendly on the surface, but under it you'll always wonder why I led you to believe I was in Christchurch. And I have no intention ever of explaining ... so don't think we're about to become friendly so you can pry.'

(There, that ought to set him back!)

His voice was urbane, his eyes shrewd. 'Oh, I have a pretty fair idea of your reason.'

Priscilla coloured hotly.

He said, 'Oh, don't look so guilty. I was severe with you, I admit. But who am I to judge? You've obviously got your personal affairs into a snarl, but I *think* you've got enough strength of character to unravel them. Don't let me down on that.'

She hadn't the faintest idea what he was talking about. That had been a blush of embarrassment, not guilt, when for one humiliating moment she'd thought he'd guessed at the attraction he had for her. But it seemed he suspected her of something else. Pity, but he'd just have to go on thinking it.

They walked on in a silence a little strained till they came to the chalet. It stood like an alpine home, surrounded by cedars, larches, pines. A low curved wall, made out of the hillside stones, gave it a sense of privacy, of a garden of its own. Mauve and pink ivy geraniums rioted over it, and ivy, as if trying to bind it together. A small picket gate, painted in cedar colour, shut it off from the copse, and smooth water-worn stones from the river led up to the central front door.

Tubs of scarlet geraniums stood each side of the door and garden seats and alyssum and aubretia sprang from the crevices. There were fuchsias all along one side and on the other, bordering a side path, were all the shrubs and trees that would be a glory come spring, almond, cherry, crab-apple, spindle-berry, forsythia, spiraea, peach, prunus, lilac, may-blossom.

A breeze sprang up, ruffled the leaves of the larches, and in front of them as they opened the gate drifted and danced the silvery balls of the thistles, suspended in the air. 'Why the Thistledown House particularly?' asked Priscilla.

'That was Uncle Manuel. Like all gardeners, he waged continual war on thistles and dandelions, but said their great compensation was the touch of magic they gave to autumn. So he thought they'd like to spend their autumn years here, their thistledown days.'

Priscilla's voice wasn't quite steady. 'But they didn't quite reach them . . . at least not together.'

'No, but so much of Manuel is here that when the time comes for Rosina to move in, she'll feel as if he really does share it with her. You see, he was a writer too, of garden books. So he had his study here. Rosina has always filled Jesmond Dene with people, some lame dogs. This gave Manuel the solitude he needed.

'He loved the old house, of course. He was born in it, but liked to think that if it proved too big, in the end, they wouldn't have to move away. A pity their children weren't able to settle here, but their careers took them away, though they all come home when they can. But the years are bound to catch up on Rosina soon. Manuel said to me not long before he died, "I've a feeling you'll be the one to live in Jesmond Dene, Barnabas. I'll trust you to pick someone kindred for my Rosina." '

Priscilla found herself unable to reply to that. The poignancy of it got her by the throat. Rosina, battling on in a house too large for her, with a garden soon to be beyond her physical strength, not wanting to sell to strangers, longing to retire to Thistledown, with its memories of Manuel, and not being able to bottle up her dislike of Melisande. But you couldn't expect a man to marry to please his aunt!

She swallowed, said, 'Manuel was born here, you said? How strange. I thought Rosina must have been.'

'Why?'

'Because of its name . . . and your name and hers. Lockhart is a name associated with Newcastle-upon-Tyne in Northumberland, and Jesmond Dene is one of its beauty spots. Yet it's Rosina who's your aunt, not Manuel your uncle.'

'In the early days this was simply called the Dene Homestead, because of Liberty Dene just up the road. Manuel tacked the Jesmond on because of his wife's connection with Newcastle. She was born here not long after her folk left the Tyneside. My grandfather emigrated as a young man and started a small store. But how come you know so much about the Tyneside?'

Priscilla stopped to sniff at a Picardy rose, with its delicate blend of cream and pink. 'Because my grandfather came from there too. I sat at his feet enthralled as he told me his tales of the great Roman Wall, of the fish-wives, the taty-engines, the dockyards. I grew up steeped in the history of the Tyneside. So it's been a great talking-point for Rosina and me.'

'Has she told you how she met Manuel?'

'No, but she said she'd known him from childhood.'

Barnabas was absent-mindedly removing dead heads from the hollyhock that grew beside the front door. 'She was visiting with her parents in the village and wandered. She got lost. She was only seven. It was so hot and she got so thirsty. The button came off her shoe and it raised a blister slipping up and down. She shuffled along in the dust, crying, then she saw the wall and knew there was a house some-where. But the wall was too high to climb and when she came to the gate it was solid and high too and she sat down in the dust and lifted up her voice and bawled.

'Manuel was fifteen, and was pruning trees inside, so he rushed out and rescued her. He took her in to his mother, who mopped her up and gave her a cooky and a cold drink. And they found out where she was visiting and rang up and asked if she could stay to tea, and the families became great friends.

'Manuel and his father thought they'd like their lane to be more hospitable in future to hot and tired children and adults, so they knocked part of the wall down and moved it back behind the chestnut and instead of the high wooden gates, they put those beautiful wrought iron ones to give a view of the garden and house. Lovely, aren't they? End of story.'

'Not really,' said Priscilla. 'Don't you know it should —and did—end with: "And they lived happily ever after"?' She paused, then added with a light in her eyes he'd never seen there before, 'Oh, I've just realised ... I could incorporate this ... the lost child shuffling in the dust and heat, the tree and its shade just out of reach ... in a story. The thick gates that shut her out, and now that delicate tracery of wrought iron against the brilliancy of the fuchsias along the drive, and the octagonal seat round the chestnut. Oh, how marvellous! Here's a whole new world of inspiration opening before me. I wonder, oh, how I wonder, if Rosina would mind if I used it.'

'Knowing my aunt, I'd say she'd be enchanted. It will be good for you to get absorbed in something like this. It will occupy your mind. Otherwise——'

She looked at him curiously. 'Otherwise what?'

He seemed to hesitate, then, 'Otherwise you might find this existence a little boring when the novelty wears off.'

She had a distinct impression he'd been going to say something else. But it might be stupid to ask. Second thoughts were often wiser, and they'd just stopped hostilities. She said instead. 'It must have been lovely for Rosina to grow up hero-worshipping Manuel—I expect that's all it was to start with—then loving him and being loved in return. How idyllically some people's romances go!'

His voice, she thought, sounded a little rough and impatient when he answered. 'Well, it's easy to imagine an idyll in other folks' lives. But who's to know? They may have had quite a stormy courtship for all we know. I've never heard anything about that, but Manuel mayn't have thought a girl of fourteen much when he was twenty-two. Rosina might have loved him hopelessly for years. He might have had several fancies while she was growing up. That would be tough on her. Her affections are boundless and deep.'

He didn't know what he was doing to Priscilla, all un-knowing that the girl at his side had longings too.

He gave a short rather embarrassed laugh. 'You'll think me a romantic. Well, I am, at that, where my aunt is con-cerned. Our mother was desperately ill for six months once, in hospital, so Dad brought us out here. She just lavished affection on us.' He laughed again. 'Anyway, perhaps Manuel was the one to find the going hard. Rosina had mischief in her, so what she was like when young, goodness knows. And even if they always cared for each other, it needn't necessarily have been ideal then. Of course it's pleasant always to have a partner for certain functions ... but that often leads girls into looking for a life-partner too soon, and if a few years elapse before one dawns on their horizons— by the time they're twenty-five or so, they think of them-selves as old maids and snatch at any chance of happiness, instead of just waiting for the fulness of time.'

Priscilla stared at him. 'Why, you speak as if you had some vitally personal stake in this. I hope you don't think me inquisitive, but it sounds to me as if something like this has happened to someone you care deeply about, like a favourite sister or cousin or something. As if you thought she'd settled for less than the ideal. But it's very hard sometimes to see what another person sees in another. I was thinking of this just recently, when I came across a quotation by Barrie: "Love is not blind; it is an extra sense that shows us that which is most worthy of regard." What do you think of that?'

He said slowly, his eyes fixed on hers, 'I think it's fine, and ought to be remembered, but I was thinking of some-thing very different—of someone letting herself care where she shouldn't. Oh, I know the forbidden has a potent charm of its own, but fences aren't always meant to be rushed ... or taken away.'

Priscilla felt vastly uncomfortable. It must be a family problem. It was rather nice of him to say as much as this. But she mustn't encourage his confidence. Sometimes people

confided in you, then afterwards regretted it and resented
the one to whom they'd opened out. She moved abruptly,
said, 'Shall we go in? I don't want to leave Rosina too
long.'

However, when he unlocked the door and they stepped
in, she forgot all sense of time. They went straight into a
large room in the A-shaped house, with a polished cork-like
floor and bright sheepskin rugs scattered on it in marigold,
brown, and natural shades. The far end was almost all glass
and looked into a dimness of trees that made you feel you
were living in a wood. The beamed ceiling rose into the
apex of the A-frame, and on either side a spiral staircase
in light polished wood on wrought iron curves led up to
wooden balconies off which opened two rooms.

Barnabas pointed to the one on the right. 'They were
guest-rooms, for Rosina and Manuel's grandchildren.
There's one bedroom on the left here and Manuel's study.
Come up and see. There's a bathroom on each balcony
and of course you can see the kitchen's open plan, tucked
behind the breakfast bar that separates it from the lounge.'

The bedroom had a low wide bed, the headboard framed
with well-filled bookshelves, and its window looked across
a curve of the brook to sunlit fields and the final gentle
curve of Liberty Hill where it sloped to the plain.

Then he opened the door of Manuel's study and Priscilla
gave a cry of delight. 'What a darling room!' and stepped in.
Her hands were clasped in front of her, her coral lips
slightly parted, her eyes shining. The two smallish casement windows peered out from the overhang to the same
sunlit fields and hill view, but here could be seen an old-
fashioned haystack and a couple of oat-stacks, symmetric-
ally crowned; sheep grazed round them and beyond
they could see the line of the Maungatuas stretching far
south.

Under the window was a large leather-topped desk, worn
and shabby in a harmonious sort of way. The blotter was
virgin, the top almost bare save a row of garden books in

a book-trough. On one side was a small rosewood desk that looked as if Rosina might use it. There were a couple of easy chairs, and a pair of low wooden steps to reach up to the top shelves of the books that lined the other three walls, except for gaps of plain wall where selections of watercolours were grouped.

They were delicately and exquisitely done, half a dozen studies of fuchsias, one of azaleas so vivid it almost seemed as if by stepping back into this room, time had flashed back to spring; there was one of cinerarias looking like purple amethysts and blue sapphires under shadowy trees, some sketches of pussywillow buds, silver birch catkins, cedar cones, sycamore keys.

'Oh, I love this,' said Priscilla in delight. 'Did Manuel use these in his garden books? If so I wish I'd seen some of his books. I wonder why I never have.'

Before he could answer she'd turned to another panel of wall hung with pictures. 'Why, it must be a local artist ... these are of Jesmond Dene itself. Here's the Thistledown House ... how enchanting! There's the lane, with the wall that was moved and the seat. It should have had the small Rosina shuffling along. Oh, how silly of me ... the seat wasn't there then. Who *is* the artist, Barnabas?'

She moved in as she spoke to peer at the thin black line of signature, and as he laughed, she read aloud, 'Barnabas Lockhart! It's you. How amazing!'

'Why amazing? Can't a draper like to fiddle round with pencil and paper too?'

'I didn't mean it that way. I meant amazing I never knew. I've lived in Dunedin all my life. Barnabas, this isn't amateur stuff. You must exhibit and sell. How have I missed you?'

He shook his head. 'It's just been a hobby. I've not exhibited. Time is my bugbear. The shop and estate take so much.'

She said warmly, 'It's no less than criminal to let a gift

like this remain largely anonymous. Other people should be given the chance to see it.'

'I do a few pictures for friends. I had great satisfaction in having them accepted for Uncle Manuel's books.'

'So you're a professional ... and here am I being rather patronising as if I'd discovered you! But you've already been published.'

'Don't apologise—I like it. I mean, you admired them before you knew who'd painted them. When I was a youngster and Mother and Dad used to show visitors my work, I used to squirm. It puts people on the spot, like authors' friends feeling they ought to like their books. Tastes differ so.'

'M'm. But if anyone didn't like these their taste would be at fault. It would be tantamount to disliking gardens and I've never yet met anyone who did.'

Priscilla walked across to the desk, laid a caressing hand upon its surface. Barnabas Lockhart said, 'You feel you could write here?'

'Yes, not just solitude in which to type, but the stimulation of Rosina's personality and all the unexpected quirks that life with children brings. I don't think anyone could write in a hermit-like existence. In fact I've heard writers say they achieved their best work in the midst of family crises and crowded days, because they have the stimulation of pitting their wits against that arch-enemy, Time.' She looked at him, chuckled. 'Although I said I'd felt I was meant to come here, there were a few moments this afternoon when I could have wished myself at Timbuktu, but not any more.'

His eyes were more serious than hers. 'Like I say, given time, most situations resolve themselves. I'd like to think your work here absorbed you, kept you from wanting to go in to your sister's place too often.'

Something in his voice chilled Priscilla's eagerness. 'I can't cut them off completely. I'd hurt them. Despite all, there is a strong family bond between us. They'll come out here to see me sometimes, of course.'

He nodded. 'But as far as possible make it as a family. If you were on your own, you could weaken. I still think if you'd been a couple of hundred miles away in Christchurch, it could have been better for you. For you and ... all concerned. No sudden impulses, no unguarded moments that way.'

It hurt. As if he thought she'd done Clarice great harm by letting her lean on her sister. She said sturdily, 'I won't weaken. I've realised I must live my own life and they must live theirs. After this, when the children go back home, I won't take Rosina's kind offer of living here. I'll probably take off.'

It really stabbed her to have him agree to that. Horrible, horrible Barnabas to so take the gilt off the gingerbread. He looked at her, said, 'Priscilla, perhaps I sound harsh, but——'

At that moment the four children arrived in, helter-skelter, and shouted up from below, 'Can we come up? We want to show Nerolie.'

Priscilla was glad. She didn't want to quarrel again with Rosina's nephew. 'Yes, come on up. I've been looking at the study. I'm trying to write children's books and I'll do some work here in school hours when Aunt Rosina is on her feet again.'

Nerolie's eyes were astar. 'How super to know someone who likes children enough to write for them. Are any printed yet?'

'Just two or three short stories in Christmas Annuals. I've got them with me if you'd like to read them. But take great care of them.'

Alicia broke in. 'She'll have to read them here. Her parents forbid her to read in bed. She has to have her light out when she gets into bed. I call that downright cruel!'

Barnabas said, 'Alicia, that's hardly fair. Nerolie may be allowed to stay up to watch television longer than you. You remember how your parents cut your reading-time down if you've stayed up later to see something special. Alicia, I absolutely forbid you to say anything about it to either Mr or Mrs Palmerston. Your passion for reform is a menace to your friends. Now, have a look over Thistledown, and then I'm going to run Nerolie back to the village. I suppose your mother knows you're here, Nerolie?'

Alicia, of course, answered. 'She does, because we saw her outside the school, but she wouldn't care anyway.'

Barnabas sighed. 'Come on . . . have a peep in here, then cut across to the other balcony and see the rooms there. Then outside. Miss Marchant, watch that floor, it's highly polished.'

'*We* call her Priscilla,' observed Alicia.

'I expect I will away from the shop,' said Barnabas. 'Right . . . Priscilla, do you want anything for dinner from the store?'

It sounded so domesticated Priscilla's ruffled feelings subsided. 'No, thanks. I sliced beans from the garden and peeled the potatoes just after lunch and the casserole's been in for ages. I hope you like plain old casserole of stewing steak.'

'I do. What's for dessert?'

'Rhubarb crumble, I think. It's quick and easy. Plenty in the garden.'

'Right, kids, we'll go and pick it, and wash it, then take Nerolie home.'

Nerolie said wistfully, 'It sounds lovely. If I can stay to tea another night, would you make it? I get so tired of rice and tapioca and sago.'

Priscilla said drily, 'Well, I'm very fond of all those too, but they'd take too long to make tonight. You can come Tuesday. I'll ring your mother.'

She thought Barnabas a bit mean not allowing the others to accompany him. When he returned he took Priscilla aside. 'I should watch Alicia's new protégée if I were you. Mrs Palmerston had the place in remarkable order considering they moved in only last week. She asked me into the kitchen as she was making a lemon soufflé and didn't want it to flop. Nerolie scuttled off. I think she puts it on a bit. I don't want you imposed upon.'

He redeemed himself by taking the children round a mile or two of country roads in the new car, and of initiating the boys into the refinements of the up-to-the-minute gadgets. He enjoyed his meal, carried his aunt out for it, told the children they were to help with the dishes and departed to return to the shop.

Priscilla felt lost when he'd gone and took herself to task for it. She'd given up her job to get away from him and the fact that he'd turned up at Jesmond Dene as practically a member of the family mustn't undermine her resolution to cut herself away from all contact with him eventually.

CHAPTER FIVE

THEY saw rather a lot of Nerolie the next ten days, but Priscilla was glad. She felt it kept Alicia from going out visiting other homes, and that relieved her because she preferred to keep that adventurous child under her own eye.

Rosina was up and about again and no lasting damage seemed to have been done to the leg. Barnabas had left them alone, for which Priscilla told herself she was devoutly glad, apart from phoning his aunt every day at some time. They were having an end-of-February sale at the shop to speed the departing summer and its fashions on its way, and he was busy on the estate getting lambs away. There'd been a strike at the freezing works earlier and it was a confounded nuisance as the lambs were now getting too fat for export.

She had little conversation with him, turning the phone over to Rosina as quickly as possible always. One morning though, phoning from the shop, he asked, 'Have you finished that story for children you were busy on? Are you starting the one about Jesmond Dene and Thistledown House yet?'

'Not quite, but I'm preparing. I've jotted down numerous small inspirations as they've occurred to me and I'm still studying masses of names to find one that just suits the little-girl-lost theme. By the way, Rosina said you had the very snap Manuel took of her the day she was lost. I thought it might give me an idea of what she was wearing. It's so important to get the period right for describing. Would it be any trouble to mail it to us?'

'I'll do better than that, I'll bring it out. I've something else to bring you may find interesting. There's just one stipulation. If you don't care for the idea, you aren't to feel obliged to use it. What appeals to one doesn't necessarily appeal to another.'

Her tone warmed. 'That's very good of you. When you write, even just a beginning writer like me, people do tend to come along with ideas that thrill them but don't spark off anything to me. But I've a feeling that——' She stopped, embarrassed by what she'd nearly said ... that she felt anything *he* might produce was bound to inspire her.

'Go on, Priscilla. You've a feeling that what?'

'Oh, nothing really. Just that as you gave me the idea of the limping little girl and the inhospitable too-high fence, you might give me another.'

'Well, it's not that exactly, but wait till tomorrow. I'm taking the morning off, so we won't get sidetracked with the children. Is Aunt Rosina still improving?'

'I can see her through the window, pacing the paths between her standard fuchsias. There are a couple of friendly fantails flirting around her. She lifts up each hanging bell with such a tender touch, as if she can't communicate with it when it droops so pendulously. What a pity you don't do figure drawing, it would be delightful to sketch her unawares, doing just that, with the fantails poised in flight above her. You could call it *My Lady of the Fuchsias* and exhibit it. I think the titles of pictures adds to their interest for the viewers.'

'That's a slant I've not thought of till now. You've given me something to think about. That's with you being a writer, I suppose. Priscilla, how about your own problem? Are you finding it easier to keep away, to withdraw a little?'

He sounded kindly, not censorious as before. 'Yes, I did what you said, pleaded being extremely busy. Roger rang me one night, and as Clarice and the youngsters were out, we had a long chat. He thinks they've grown closer together already, more of a family unit, complete in themselves. This is good.'

'Indeed it's good. And it wasn't too painful for you, knowing this?'

Priscilla felt surprised. 'No, I wouldn't let myself be hurt by that, Barnabas. I'm not in the least a possessive type. Besides, I've too much to think about and do. I'd have felt the break more had I got another flat further away. I'd have time to miss—oh, what shall I say?—the old bonds. One gets used to thinking of people as indissolubly part of one's life, but a complete break like this was necessary, and the way it dropped into my lap when I needed it most seemed heaven-sent. Perhaps you'll like that expression better than my saying soulfully that I thought I was led here.'

'Priscilla?'

'Yes?'

'I apologise for that. I was taken off balance and in a flaming temper that day because you'd lied to me. When I'd got your letter I admired you tremendously for making what I thought was a clean break and therefore despised you just as much when I found you still within easy access, so I reacted rather too strongly. I still don't understand it, but I give you credit for withstanding temptation. I expect it *did* seem like a leading when you found Aunt in such a predicament and so obviously in need of someone like you. Well, I'll see you both tomorrow morning. I'll stay for lunch, but I must be back at the shop by one-thirty. Goodbye for now.'

Priscilla stood by the phone pondering what he'd said for some time. He'd inadvertently overheard her discussion with Roger and had seemingly condemned her a little for the situation. He had imagined her as the bossy spinster sister, throwing her weight about, making herself indispensable to the family, thus weakening the unit of husband, wife, children. It hurt a little that he had assumed the fault to be mainly hers. If only he could have known how she'd longed to live her own life, how clinging Clarice and Mother had been. But if one attempted to explain, it sounded like a weak excuse and disloyal.

But . . . her spirits lifted. He was coming out here, partly to see his aunt, but surely mainly to see her with this idea he'd given birth to. She hoped, with an intensity that amazed her, that it was one she could accept and work on. She went in search of Rosina, to tell her Barnabas was going to spend tomorrow morning with them.

She was now among the lilies and roses. The Michaelmas daisies were thick with bees, the tall spikes of the Canterbury Bells were glories of pink and purple, so were the perennial phlox, and lavender and mignonette bordered the paths.

Rosina looked well and serene, the hazel eyes sparkling over cheeks pinker than usual. The company had done her good, and Alicia hadn't got up to any really outrageous pranks, apart from gate-crashing on old Mr Crimmon, who was getting past looking after his too-extensive aviary, and telling him he ought to be ashamed of himself for not cleaning the cages more often.

Oddly enough, the old eccentric had taken it quite well after their initial confrontation, a clanging exchange overheard by an agitated neighbour who thought he'd eat her. She'd told Priscilla she'd thought the old man had been pleased he was merely attacked for being lazy, and not told he was getting past it and ought to get rid of them. The upshot was that now Alicia went there twice a week to help him with the task. It kept her crusading passions occupied a little and left her less time for mothering—or smothering—the pathetic Nerolie.

'Has your nephew said anything to you on the phone about some idea he has for me to write about, Rosina?' she asked.

'He has, the dear boy. He had to ask me about one or two things. But you aren't to try to pump me, Priscilla. It would lessen the impact his notion has upon you, if you had a preliminary run-down. No, not one question. Look, Priscilla ... summer isn't quite over yet, but here's the first autumn crocus out, over by the stone fence. It's so dry there you wouldn't think anything could thrive, but out of that parched earth comes this frail beauty ... all silvery cyclamen. And there are the peacock-tiger lilies, in all their glory blooming just for a day.'

Had there ever been a summer like this? Priscilla gloated on the prodigality of leaf and bloom and fragrance. Masses of hydrangeas forming walks, montbretia greedily filling the empty spaces, daisies of every shape and hue, pansies and forget-me-nots, campanulas and aubrietia, geraniums and blue gentian.

She found it hard to conceal her singing happiness from Rosina. She felt as if it must be marked upon her face and Rosina was too astute, not to say outspoken, but she said nothing and looked nothing. Archness or surmise would have spoiled this for her. It was merely an interested gesture on Barnabas's part, but it was something to look forward to, dropped in her lap by kindly gods, as the ancients used to say. She'd tried to get away from him but it hadn't come off. So she might as well enjoy what she couldn't avoid.

She planned the meal she would give him and prepared it the night before. She simmered lamb sweetbreads for an hour, drained them ready to be egged and crumbed, then fried at the last moment; cooked some of the garden beans, green and tender, and put them in the fridge to be tossed up with orange and cucumber slices, walnuts and olives for a salad. She blanched chips ready to re-heat, and made, under Rosina's instructions, his favourite boysenberry tart, and cheese straws to have coffee with later.

She listened to a forecast of good weather and woke to birdsong and a morning so still not even the tips of the pines were murmuring. The sunlight slanted in her small casements and sunbeams danced in the shaft of light.

When the children had gone off to school and the dishes had been washed and beds made, she changed into cinnamon brown silky slacks and donned an artist's smock she loved to work in, it was so loose and cool for sitting at the typewriter. It was tussore-coloured and splashed with red poppies, blue cornflowers, and green leaves. She left it open at her brown throat. Her slim brown feet were bare but for sandals little more than thongs.

She was glad she'd resisted the temptation to dress up for him, but Rosina's reaction couldn't have been greater had she worn one of Lockhart's more exclusive models. 'Oh, Priscilla, I've never seen you look more beautiful. Those brighter colours are just lovely on you . . . like a splash of red on a robin's breast in England. Yet it's such a workman-like garb. The day's going to be very hot, but Manuel's study is shady with the trees all about it. He planned it that way, said he couldn't work in heat, because there was little you could do to reduce that, but you could always warm it in winter with a huge fire. He always burned the aromatic logs, peach wood from the prunings, apple-wood, gum leaves.'

Priscilla could almost smell them. 'Oh, Rosina, how I wish I could have known your Manuel. Though I almost feel I do since working in his study. It takes me all my time not to keep dipping into his garden books over there. Oh, I do wish my father could have read them. He so delighted in that sort of thing. The other day I almost ached to share them with him.'

Rosina's great hazel eyes lit up her small face. 'But he did read the last one, just before he died. I gave him a signed copy Manuel had left a stack of. Seth read it and came straight out here to tell me how much he'd enjoyed it. Oh, he brought papers out for me to sign, but there was no doubt why he'd made a point of it. Did you never see it among your father's books?'

'No. Perhaps it was left at the office. He died so suddenly. I could ask the partners if it's still there, I'd love to have it.'

'If not, you shall have its twin. I took your father over to Manuel's study, so he should see where he'd written it. There was a good deal about the chalet in his book.'

Priscilla clasped her hands together in the gesture of delight she so often used. 'Oh, Rosina, this means so much to me—to know my father actually knew the room I'll be working in. For some reason I've had a spell of missing him horribly since coming out here, thinking how I'd like him to see this place. For so long after he died Mother couldn't seem to pick up, then Clarice lost Geoff and we had the flat built in her property, and there were so many details in the way of business to be attended to, and Andrew to get off to Oxford, that I found myself resenting the fact that I scarcely had time to mourn him. Can you understand that? I felt it was his due to be sadly missed, but time caught up with me and rolled over me.'

A voice other than Rosina's answered her, Barnabas's voice from the open doorway. 'I can understand that, and not only understand it but like it. I've heard Rosina say what a fine man Seth Marchant was, what integrity and kindness there was in him, and I think he did deserve to be missed and grieved for.'

She turned, unclasping her hands, feeling warmth in her face, and looking both shy and pleased. Barnabas came across to them, said, 'Don't blush, Priscilla, though it suits you. You seldom do it, or show it. Perhaps because you're such a brown girl. I know it was an intimate conversation between two people and it *is* disconcerting to have a third horn in, but I liked it, and wanted to.'

Rosina saved Priscilla the necessity of reply. 'Of course you did, Barnabas. You were never one to bottle up your feelings, so you don't mind showing them and you appreciate other people having them. Priscilla expresses hers so beautifully it's a delight to have her here.'

He grinned, bent to kiss his aunt, said, 'I don't suppose you'd ever believe that my Miss Marchant was so prim and proper, so everything the well-trained secretary ought to be, that she got on my nerves. I thought she didn't have any red blood in her veins at all.'

'I don't believe it,' said Rosina fondly. 'I always thought you were perceptive, you horrible boy. Anybody ought to be able to see what Priscilla is like.'

Priscilla came to his rescue. She laughed. 'The fault was

mine. I'd heard he wanted a secretary to be more or less a machine, not to get involved with him personally at all, so I acted accordingly.'

'It was awful,' said Barnabas with relish. 'She smiled politely at my jokes, like someone humouring a kid showing off, had an inflection in her voice like an icicle if I complimented her on her appearance, and told me she preferred to stay Miss Marchant, not to be called Priscilla. It was most traumatic.'

Rosina giggled. 'I'd like to have seen it. The irrepressible Barnabas being put in his place!'

'And,' he continued, 'whenever Melisande drifted in, I was made to feel I was wasting time. Talk about a watch-dog!'

'Well,' said Rosina, 'you're wasting time now. Over to Thistledown with you. I slipped over earlier and put some morning tea ready for you in a flask so you'd not feel you had to come back here to have it with me. I don't want to be delayed either. I want to get all the lower dead heads of the gladioli off.'

Barnabas had an attaché case with him. He picked it up and they set off through the morning sunlight. Just before they reached the bridge he looked to the right, said, 'That's one of my favourite sights year after year . . . Aunt Rosina's little triangular bed of farewell-summers.'

Priscilla looked. 'Aren't they asters? Oh, is that their common name? I always like the common names. Like snow-in-summer, instead of cerastium tomentosum and columbines or granny-bonnets instead of aquilegia.'

'Yes, and Ladies' Pincushions instead of scabious and Love-in-a-Mist for nigella.'

How kindred he was! They found themselves in Manuel's study. Priscilla had typescript in neat piles all over the desk and she gathered these up now and put them aside on a small table. Then she turned to her former boss and said, 'Now . . . your idea, Barnabas. I promise to tell you if it lights no fires for me.'

'Well, first, you know that Spring Catalogue we're thinking of bringing out in August? I had a real inspiration about
that. This new girl will take time to work into her job and
it's a bit outside her ken. You did our autumn one a few
months ago, and added a subtle something in your revision
that made it much more than a run-of-the-mill one. I can
see now it betrays your knack with words. Can't think how
I didn't recognise it. So I wondered if you'd make time here
to work on this one. You could keep a record of your hours,
and the pay, of course, would be higher per hour than the
usual rate. It would help us and it would help you too,
financially, now you're on a lower wage.'

Disappointment flooded Priscilla and almost betrayed
her. She had been looking for something inspirational,
something to do with that which lay dearest to her heart.
This was merely commercial. But it was a kind gesture. She
schooled her features into appreciation. She felt mystified,
too, because what he'd said over the phone had led her to
believe he was going to suggest a story-line to her.

She said, 'That's extremely good of you. I'll gladly do it.
But I'm quite happy to take just a nominal wage from
Rosina, because it gives me the chance of working an hour
or two a day on my own thing. And Roger has succeeded in
getting a good tenant for my flat. But give me a deadline
for the catalogue and I'll produce it.'

'Splendid. Now for something else—your stories. You
liked my illustrations in Uncle Manuel's books, didn't you?
How about this?'

She'd never seen him diffident before. At Lockhart's, as
befitting a managing director, he was decisive, knowledge-
able, confident. She stared at him as he put his case on the
desk, drew out some cartridge paper and held it out to her.
'It's just this.'

He kept it at arm's length for her to study. She caught
in her breath. *Just this!* She said it to herself, silently, then
aloud: '*Just this*. Barnabas! Oh, how can you say such a
thing? It—it's quite unbelievably beautiful. It's something

that was beginning to jell in my own mind ... that's why I
wanted the snap. Oh, to think I said what a pity you
couldn't draw figures! I spoke out of ignorance. Oh, it's so
perfect. Like having a dream as dim as a cobweb in a dark
corner suddenly outlined for you with hoar-frost, crystal-
clear and sparkling. And the perfect title.Why didn't I think
of that name myself? None of mine were right.'

The lettering above what was obviously intended for a
dust-jacket was exquisitely done. It said simply:

AMBROSINA
LOST
AND
FOUND

and the A of the Ambrosina was a miniature chalet. There
was the little Ambrosina in the garments children wore the
year the First World War broke out, trotting along a dusty
lane, dejection in every line, and a forbidding wall reaching above her, keeping the shade of the trees from her, and
an equally forbidding and inhospitable pair of gates set in
the middle.

He said, 'I made Rosina promise not to even hint. I asked
her permission to use her full name. It is right, isn't it? It
gave me the greatest satisfaction. You gave me the inspiration for it. This was my first love, of course, what I wanted
most to do. But I felt if my father could give his time to
commerce for the sake of his staff, when all he wanted was
to run Tyne Hill full time, then I could give him the satisfaction of having me follow in his footsteps to give him a
bit more time on the estate. But I realised, when you told
me what you were hoping to do, that I shouldn't have let
this go when Manuel died. I wondered—but only if you
feel entirely happy about it—if we could collaborate in a
children's series, and try an overseas market?'

Enchantment was still upon her, in her eyes astar with
dreams, in her parted lips, her quickened breathing. She
couldn't know Barnabas Lockhart was looking at his one-

time cool and disdainful secretary and wondering how he could ever have dubbed her a plainish brown sort of girl.

Priscilla shook her head a little as if to clear it, said, 'I still can't quite believe it. How can you say *if* I feel entirely happy about it? How could I be anything else? To have the story *and* the illustrator dropped into my lap. It's a dream-come-true. I have a tentative contact with a publisher of children's books. The ones who put out the annual a couple of my stories were accepted for. He said he liked my touch, and if I launched out into any larger individual work, he'd be interested to see it. Nothing more than that except he did add that if I provided the text, they could find an artist to illustrate it, but it's always better to submit as a finished product, and to have someone like you do it would take away the very real dread of getting an illustrator who wouldn't quite capture one's own mental images. Oh, Barnabas, the *un*-horrible, I feel like A. A. Milne or Beatrix Potter, on the verge of a career!'

The broad face with its square chin and bluest of eyes was very close to hers. He said, with an upward quirk of his mouth, 'Let's seal that contract. I haven't any champagne, I'm afraid, partner, but . . . how about this?'

She had one delicious moment of anticipation. His hands came to her shoulders, fastened tightly, and he drew her to him, laughed down into her startled brown eyes, put his mouth on hers. She felt delight stir within her, set her heart beating rapidly, and send a feathering of emotion along her pulses. It lasted quite a few moments, then he released her and laughed. 'Well, well, who'd have thought it? The one-time cool secretary? We'd better get down to business. Not that I wouldn't like to continue, but just imagine if Aunt Rosina came in on us unexpectedly. She'd think I had an ulterior motive, nothing whatever to do with art or literature. But fortunately those stairs creak. No one will ever creep up on us unawares, I promise.'

Priscilla managed to recover herself. 'Well, I shan't worry over that. I recognise this for exactly what it is.'

His voice almost squeaked with curiosity. 'For what it is? What can you mean?'

She said it lightly, shaking her head as she might have done at an over-demonstrative child, 'It's just as well I'm not one of the designing hussies you wanted to avoid having in your office. I could have taken you seriously. That was just a spontaneous outcome of an overcharged moment of satisfaction because you'd found an outlet for your creative talent. I understand only too well. I felt the same myself. Something seemed called for. Now let's go back to business, as you say. Morning hours are so precious and so fleeting.'

His eyes were still twinkling. 'Back to normal, are we? I hardly recognised my former secretary for a few moments, but once more I see that familiar reproving glint in your eye that meant I was wasting the firm's time, and yours. Right, slave-driver, let's get down to it. No room for both of us at this desk, so what about using the big table Manuel and I used to work at? Could you outline for me a little of what you intend to write, or will I distract you?'

Priscilla wouldn't admit he could easily distract her, even if he hadn't meant it that way. They worked away and though normally she hated sharing undeveloped ideas with anyone, the fact that her written words would be enhanced by his sketches inspired her in a way never before experienced. An hour and a half had passed before they heard the stairs creak and the tap of heels.

Barnabas scowled. 'That's not Rosina's footsteps. Who the devil has she let come over?' They were sitting close, leaning over the sketches, and turned their heads as one towards the open doorway while the taps continued along the little gallery and next moment someone was framed in the doorway—Melisande Drew!

Barnabas moved his leg which brought it against Priscilla's and she was aware at once that he had tautened.

Melisande, fresh from the hairdresser's hands, looked more beautiful than ever, her silky blonde hair swept up into a superb topknot and fastened each side with a tortoiseshell comb. She wore an emerald green summer fabric suit that must have cost her a month's salary, and her complexion was exquisitely laid on.

'Well, well,' she said mockingly, her green eyes glinting, 'doesn't this look cosy? No wonder Rosina told me to be sure to knock!'

Priscilla found Barnabas had stiffened even more. 'That didn't mean a thing, Melisande. Rosina belongs to the old school, and she didn't like your going straight in when she was entertaining Georgina Gainsborough last month. She was just getting back at you for that, not that Miss Marchant and I were shut into any cosy situation. The door was open, wasn't it? And we're extremely busy working on the Spring Catalogue which, to my relief, she's consented to continue. My new secretary rather blenched at the idea. So Miss Marchant, once we've got it straight, is going to work on it here in Manuel's study.'

'How very interesting ... but I wonder why you told me that your secretary had left you for a job in Christchurch? It's extremely odd, to say the least, to find her neatly tucked into the chalet and you out here working with her. Could there possibly be any credible explanation of that?'

Priscilla felt sick in the pit of her stomach. Now look what she'd involved Barnabas in! All she could do was hold her tongue and see what Barnabas came up with. He stood up, picked up the sheaf of papers they'd been working on, slid them under those of the catalogue and put a paperweight on top.

There was leashed anger beneath his drawling voice. 'Really, Melisande, how dramatic of you! It's all so simple. When I told you that, I was under the impression that Miss Marchant was seeking a position in Christchurch. Seeking, mark you, not that she'd already secured one. She wrote me from where she was staying there. The carbon copy of that letter is filed in my office, though I shouldn't think you'd have the nerve to demand to see it, but if you have, it's there, with my reply, sending her a reference to facilitate her search.

'But she changed her mind, found she didn't, after all, want to be so far away from home. Meanwhile she found out that Rosina wanted a part-time companion to help her with Zillah's children. You'll recall I was very against Rosina having them at all, but it was different if she had help, and very good at that. When Miss Marchant's sister was widowed, she practically brought up her niece and nephew. The sister's remarried since and she thought they ought to be on their own. It *is* simple, isn't it? Not in the least clandestine or sly, which was what you seemed to imply.' He allowed himself a note of angry indignation which was clever. It carried the attack into the enemy's camp.

Melisande blinked, seemed to think it acceptable fleetingly, then said triumphantly, 'Oh come, I'm not green. What girl would give up the sort of position she had for a paltry job like this? That's asking me to look gullible!'

His voice took on a cold edge again. 'Not to look gullible, just believing. You've known me long enough to trust me. Miss Marchant is a writer. She's had quite a bit of freelance stuff accepted. She had a ambition to attempt something bigger. This gives her the time, a job like this, mainly looking after the youngsters when they're home from school, and the chalet is an ideal place to work in. Not even a phone for interruptions ... that is when her former boss doesn't impose on her.'

The brilliant green eyes fixed themselves on Priscilla who still sat at the desk, trying and succeeding in looking cool and unconcerned, playing with a ballpoint. Melisande's voice was contemptuous. 'Do you really mean to tell me you'd give up a well-paid job for the airy-fairy chance of making a living, *some day*, out of scribbling?'

Priscilla couldn't help it. She smiled in what she hoped was a maddeningly superior fashion and said, 'It's been done before. It's all in the best tradition, isn't it? To starve in a garret while you attempt to make your name. I admit it was good to have Mr Lockhart ask me to do the catalogue. That gives me extra, but I've let my flat for a very good price so I'm not exactly down to my last dollar. Though I've no need to explain to you. It's my own business, but I wouldn't like to think that my being here in any way upset a personal relationship for my very kind employer.'

Melisande looked temporarily taken aback, then rallied. 'You *couldn't* upset it, but you must allow it seemed very odd, especially the secrecy. Barney, why didn't you tell me when I commented on your change of secretary that Miss Marchant had come back to Dunedin and you'd asked her to help Rosina?'

He did the best thing, burst out laughing. 'You'll never believe *this*. I hadn't the faintest idea she was here. Rosina took the children earlier than expected, slyboots that she is, and didn't let on to me. Not till she got them and Miss Marchant settled in, rang me and told me sweet as you like that the daughter of her late solicitor was staying with her to help. I came out here to tick Rosina off and just about went up in smoke when my former secretary came tripping down the steps.'

Melisande looked from one to the other suspiciously. 'Then that's odd too, Miss Marchant and your aunt conspiring together to keep it dark from you. Why?'

He seized on that. 'Exactly, why should they have done that? The answer is that they didn't. You know how vague Rosina is. She told Miss Marchant that her horrible nephew, Barnabas, objected to her taking the children. You know that at the shop I'm just Mr Peter Lockhart Junior, and even you never called me Barney in front of her. You just flung your usual endearments round. Evidently Miss Marchant was all worked up when she knew the horrible Barnabas was coming out . . . but it was nothing to how she felt when *I* got out of the car. The confrontation we had then was nothing to the one *we're* having at the moment. I was practically as suspicious as you, expecting her to be settling into a new job two hundred miles away. Not that Rosina knew we had a go at each other. She was confined to bed and we didn't want to upset her too much. I just teased her about pinching my secretary.'

Melisande said slowly, 'It's so crazy I suppose it's got to be true.'

Priscilla said warmly, 'Oh, I'm glad. That's big of you. I was beginning to feel like the spanner in the works.' She giggled, which was a good thing. 'I'd formed the most shocking picture of this formidable nephew of Rosina's. I thought of him as hating children, as pompous, portly, prosperous, or skinny, sarcastic, sneering. Then my perfectly ordinary boss turned up, but for one horrible moment when he accused me of being devious about the Christchurch job-hunting, I wished he *had* been the horrible nephew. He took some convincing that Rosina and I were both innocent of any deception.'

Melisande sat down on the arm of a chair. 'Well, as long as my mind wasn't the only suspicious one, I'm satisfied. I wanted to see you about the barbecue for Saturday, darling. As I'm on duty at two, when the office told me you could be reached here, I decided to run out to see you.'

Priscilla took the point. She said, 'I must go and start the lunch. You'll stay, won't you, Miss Drew? I know Rosina will want you to, and there'll be plenty for an extra.'

'Good idea,' said Barnabas. 'We'll have it early, because I mustn't be away from the shop too long, and we've gone as far as we can with the catalogue for now. Work on it till you've knocked it into shape, then if I haven't time to run out here to check it before the final typing, you might drop into the office with it. In fact that would be better, so the heads of the departments can check those alterations.'

Very clever, stressing the fact that this working together was only for mutual convenience. Priscilla went out into the near noonday sun and over to the house.

She showed no evidence of strain to Rosina. Better for her not to know there had been any challenging and unpleasant moments. Rosina would be partisan towards Priscilla, if she knew, and might even rejoice that Melisande had been put in her place, if that was the expression for it.

She felt uneasy about appearing so much the hostess, but when she suggested to Rosina that she should serve out, Rosina turned it down flat. 'I'm so happy to have you do it. Tell me when it's ready and I'll stroll over and tell them to come.'

When she was, Priscilla said, 'And by the way, Rosina, don't comment on Barnabas calling me Miss Marchant. He did it after Melisande came in, probably thinks it wiser.'

Rosina snorted. 'I won't comment, but Barnabas is a fool.' She turned back from the door, said, 'And I'm not going to say you might stay on here in the Thistledown House after the children are gone, to be company for me in my advancing years! I've felt some time that only the fact that Barnabas has always said he'd live here when he's married has been holding that one back from marrying him. She doesn't believe in all this fuss about preserving old houses. So the longer that evil day is postponed the better. I don't understand him. She dumped him once in favour of someone else, then got jilted herself. She just makes a convenience of him. I'm being catty, I'd better go and get them.'

Lunch went surprisingly smoothly. Priscilla found an exquisite pleasure in serving Barnabas with food he obviously enjoyed, though he was tactful and didn't overpraise. He must have worked out, too, that if he continued to say Miss Marchant Rosina would comment, because he said, casually, 'By the way, Melisande, you'll be out often enough while Miss Marchant is here, you'd better make it Priscilla and I'll drop the office atmosphere and do it too. Priscilla, call her Melisande.'

They smiled at each other and did. Rosina was very punctilious to Melisande, and Melisande to her, but it lacked warmth and spontaneity. When lunch was over Rosina got them all outside while she picked Melisande lilies and roses to take to the hospital, but it was a great relief when they departed in the two cars. Rosina and Priscilla washed the dishes and went across to the chalet to look at the sketches. Priscilla wanted to be very sure Rosina wouldn't mind.

'Mind, child? I'm enchanted. I hoped you would be too, and I can see you are. He's got my dress perfectly. He had the snap to go by, of course. I described the colours to him. In those days when you came from school you were put into navy-blue print frocks, with white spots. It was practically regulation. They faded horribly, because in those days navy dyes and green dyes were most unreliable. They seemed to improve after the war. Barnabas has got that washed-out look perfectly, hasn't he? What quaint styles they were, long bodices and little gathered skirts hardly longer than a frill.

'Oh, look at my copper-toed boots! Copper-toes had gone out mostly, but my parents kept to them for me because I just wouldn't stop kicking stones.'

Priscilla laughed. 'You still do it, darling. I've noticed you on the path through the copse, kicking twigs out of your way. I love your black knitted socks too, right up to your knobbly little knees. And your mushroom hat.'

'It wasn't meant to be mushroomed. I freckled easily. Mother had a milk-and-roses complexion, and never showed a blemish. I love freckles on children myself—now—but I was made to feel it was a disaster. I was never allowed out without a big panama hat with a green straw underlining, and a white elastic snapped under my chin. The brim was supposed to be flat, but I always turned it up so I could see the sky. Hasn't Barnabas done the lane beautifully? What a good thing Manuel took that snap, because it gives the right heights of the trees at that time.

'Could we sit down and go over things now so you can pick out the bits of my reminiscences that you'll want to use? You'll bring your own creativeness into it, of course. Don't hesitate to do that. But I think the factual base will be good. They're going to be small books, aren't they, that seven and eight-year-olds can hold in their tiny hands, in bed at nights?'

'I should think so. That's over to the publisher . . . when, or do I mean if, they're published?'

'They'll be published all right.'

'I should think the quality of the art work would be a big point in their favour. I'll hope to produce a text worthy of Barnabas's sketches. Oh, how mad I am to dream like this, but how I'd like to create something adults will love to read too, like Beatrix Potter or A. A. Milne. Goodness, hark at me . . . I'm developing a grandeur complex! A few rejections will bring me back to earth.'

'I remember everything about Jesmond Dene so vividly. I hope I can bring those days to life to you, and it will keep Manuel's memory alive for future generations. My sons and daughter will love to hand them on to *their* grandchildren. I was just ten in the latter stages of the war, and Manuel, when he reached eighteen, was called up. I can still see him going off down the lane with his mother and father in the trap. I wasn't allowed to go to see him off on the troop-ship. I can see him now in that new, rough khaki. He had only two months on active service when it was all over, thank God. We married ten years later, so it happened our sons were too young for the next war, so I've been a fortunate woman. Some women saw husbands go to one war, sons to the next.

'When Manuel took on landscape gardening, it was like a dream, an idyll. Hard but rewarding, and we could do it together. Then in later years he wrote his books, just three of them. It sort of crowned his life.' She looked down on the cover sketch, turned it aside, saw another with a gangling boy of fifteen coming out of the big gates, open now, to comfort a small girl in a blue print pinny, and she said, 'Oh, if only Manuel could see this!' Priscilla put her arms about the small, somehow indomitable figure and hugged it.

Rosina said, 'I was meant to get hooked up on the Wellingtonia, at the very time you sat on Manuel's bench. I'd had a bad day. Anne's letter had been held up by a strike at London Airport, so it was one of the times when I hated the distance that lies between us. But they'll be home this time next year and settled in Christchurch. Wonderful to know that a six-hour drive will bring her here, instead of having to cross the world. We're such pals. I don't know how I'd have existed when they all went overseas, without Barnabas.' She caught Priscilla's eye and laughed. 'Without dear, *horrible* Barnabas!'

Priscilla decided she must introduce a lighter note, 'You're nothing but an old fraud and I don't know why I love you, but I do, so help me. Now, I must work on the material you've just given me. Barnabas wants me to take the script of the catalogue into the office some time, and I'd like to have more done of the text for *Ambrosina* for him to work on too.'

Rosina sounded disappointed. 'He's not coming out here to work on it, then?' Then with a flash of insight she said, 'Oh, he'd just say that in front of Melisande. It won't mean a thing.' Mischief lit the hazel eyes. For an instant Priscilla could see her as a naughty seven-year-old. Then she realised something. She'd have to guard against giving Rosina any hint that she had a *tendresse* for her nephew. There was a matching glint in that twinkle. What a complication that would make! Melisande had evidently ditched Barnabas once before. No mischief must be made now. Rosina departed and Priscilla lost herself in her work. But the rapture of the morning had departed.

CHAPTER SIX

PRISCILLA found herself working fast on the catalogue—to get it out of the way, she told herself. Nevertheless, she had a suspicion that it was really because when the typing on that was complete, it would give her an excuse to visit Lockhart's.

It was therefore a surprise when only two days passed before Barnabas arrived at the chalet again. This time it was afternoon. He came charging up to the study, sat down at the table beside her. He was quite blatant about his reason. 'I thought it better to come when Melisande was on duty.'

Priscilla said as lightly as she could, 'Very wise. You won't want to upset her again.'

'It's nothing of the kind. I can't work with her around. When I can spare time from the shop without it disturbing my conscience too much, I don't want it frittered away. I missed doing this sort of thing with Manuel, though it's years ago. I've been a bit fed up with the daily grind lately. I'll be glad when Dad and Mother are back. Certainly Dad's going to semi-retire, but it takes a bit of the heat off at both the shop and Tyne Hill when we share the responsibility. I'm all set to spend a bit of time on this.'

Priscilla tried not to feel glad. She oughtn't to. But after all, why feel so guilty? She'd made a bid to get away from this man whose proximity had so much power to disturb her, but things, as Burns had said, had gone agley. There was nothing to be done about it, so why not enjoy what the Fates had given her? But what had they given her? Well, at best a satisfying working partnership, nothing more. Because Melisande had first claim on his affections, but her own life seemed linked with Barnabas Lockhart's. Their

97

names might even appear together in a publisher's contract some day, and on the spine of a book.

She found Barnabas looking at her, closely. He had an indulgent smile on his lips. 'Is that a profitable daydream? You were smiling at your thoughts. Are you weaving a few paragraphs for our book in your mind?' *Our* book.

He was surprised she'd spent all her time on the catalogue. 'I thought you wouldn't have been able to resist working on *Ambrosina*. Is the catalogue bothering you? Did you feel you must get it out of the way? Because if it's going to interfere too much with inspiration, I'll get it done at the shop somehow.'

'Oh, don't. No reason why we can't do both. I'm used to writing my verse and articles after work. I should be able to fit this in. But I can see you'd rather not tackle the adverts this afternoon. We'll work on the book today. It will refresh you for your reluctant re-entry into the commercial world.'

He chuckled. 'How neatly put! How precise. Every now and then, Miss Marchant, I can see the solicitor syndrome in you. Came from living with your father, I suppose. I noticed it as soon as you came to work for me. That's probably why I put you down as . . .'

He paused. She said wickedly, '. . . as plain and sensible!'

He gave her a scowl. 'I wasn't going to say that.'

'Perhaps neat but not gaudy would fill the bill?' Her eyes, almond-shaped under the fine dark brows, and the colour of brook stones under running water, were brimful of mischief.

'You just like seeing me squirm. I put you down as either very placid, or a little frigid.'

'But now?'

'Well, the other morning I found out very enjoyably that there was fire under the ice.'

Instinctively, she drew back a little, and her hand went to rustle their papers to remind him they were there to work.

He said, 'Let me have my say. I realise now it was because it had put your back up when Miss Wincombe said I preferred my secretaries to keep their distance, and that was fair enough. But it was good, after smarting under your almost iron rule for months, to find that after all, you still had all the feelings a woman should have.'

Priscilla sighed and was glad that in no way could he know how this was sending up her pulse rate. She said, a little scornfully, 'You're making far too much out of an excited moment two days ago. I said at the time that——'

'I know what you said. You analysed it the way the Miss Marchant I used to know would have done—a spontaneous outburst of satisfaction because I'd found an outlet for my creative talent or some such rot! Sounds like a report to be digested, marked "No follow-up" and filed away. I kissed you because you looked particularly beautiful at that moment and because I wanted to kiss you. And you shared it very nicely . . . mutually satisfying, I hope.'

'Who's analysing now?'

'I am. And much more accurately. How about agreeing?'

'How about getting on with either the catalogue or the collaborating? Otherwise I'll find I accomplish more on my own.'

He laughed in the most maddening fashion and said, 'Under that threat I give in, but that's the only reason.'

Priscilla said quite seriously, 'You ought to have another reason to keep strictly to business.'

'What reason?'

'Melisande. She was very decent when things were explained to her. I'd like it to stay that way.'

His mouth tightened just a little. 'We aren't engaged, you know. If Melisande was wearing my ring I wouldn't go round kissing other women.'

'Wouldn't you? That's good to know. But it was obvious she was a little disturbed to find you here with me.'

He laughed shortly. 'It wouldn't do Melisande any harm

to suffer a few jealous pangs. She's caused them sometimes.'

'That's nothing to do with me. Don't use me to give anyone pangs. What do you take me for?'

'I really don't know. I don't know you at all. You're so
different from what I first thought. You're full of surprises.'

'So are you. I expected to find Rosina's nephew really
horrible. But when *you* turned up it was even more ghastly.'

His eyes went keen. 'Because you'd deceived me?'

She bit her lip. Oh, why had she let the conversation
stray back to this? 'Yes. It was something way out from
my usual behaviour pattern, so I wasn't used to having my
integrity doubted, but yet I knew I deserved it. But I
thought it would make you consider me beyond the pale,
but instead——' she faltered.

'Instead?' His expression told her she'd have to finish
that.

'Instead I find you kind, magnanimous even, considering
the way I blotted my copybook. Yet all the time you have
your reservations about me.'

His eyes went grave. 'You could be right. It could be I
like you and appreciate what you're doing for my aunt
and her waifs, but at times I know it's against my better
judgment.'

'I'm sorry. I don't care for that. But I just *can't* explain
it.'

He said unexpectedly, 'Poor Priscilla, I'm grilling you
and it's hardly fair. It's quite evident that someone else is
involved and your sense of loyalty made you act out of
character.'

There was nothing she could say. He'd imagined something so far from the truth, and wild horses wouldn't drag
that out of her. So she said neither yea nor nay. Instead,
desperately, 'We really must get on with this. Mornings are
better for us. The children will be home before very long.'

'And you won't, even for this work so dear to your heart,

skip your responsibility to them? But surely Rosina can look to them for one afternoon?'

She sounded almost apologetic. 'It's just that I'm nearer their mother's age than Rosina. I feel I'm a stand-in. I think children should get a good welcome when they come in from school. It got me by the throat a little the other day when that Nerolie said quite wistfully, "You seem to like having us home. I wish *my* mother did." It must be awful for children to feel nuisances. Oh, I don't want to set myself up as a paragon, and I'd be a hypocrite if I didn't admit that often, when they're safely in bed, I find myself thanking God for the peace and quiet, but I love them to come home eager to spill out the day's history of little achievements or setbacks, nice surprises or minor disasters. They get it all out of their systems and you feel they're having a happy childhood to remember. We never know what's ahead of them and it's wonderful to have that, something nothing can take away from them. That's why I love writing things for children, because with a book even the little sick ones can find a happy hour. Mr Lockhart, we must get on.'

Their discussion seemed to have stimulated them. He started on his sketching with a will, Priscilla looked over the jottings she'd made in odd leisure moments spared from the catalogue and set about roughing them into shape. She became absorbed in the adventures of small *Ambrosina*. The fact that they were used to working together helped.

Finally, Priscilla said, 'I'll make you a cup of tea. You'll be able to get an hour or two in the shop after that. Sorry the afternoon hours don't suit so well.'

His lips twitched. 'You're at it again, Miss Marchant . . . bossing your boss. I've no intention of going back to the shop. Mr Wills has everything in hand and doesn't expect me back. That's what managers are for, to manage in the chief's absence. Besides, I'm taking you out tonight. Rosina feels it's all work and no play for you and is afraid the life might pall if you have no break away from it.'

She looked at him, said, 'And like a good little boy, you dutifully agreed to do what your aunt suggested!'

'I did nothing of the kind. Rosina only said that when I told her I was carrying you off. Don't fuss. Don't say Rosina shouldn't be on her feet too long, that you must get the dinner yourself. It's not to be anything posh. We're not going out till eight o'clock. We're spending the evening at the Manse with Elspeth and Dougal. He's my best friend, you know. They were in the shop yesterday and proposed it. They wanted us to make it dinner, but Manse life, I know, is hectic, so I said no, we'd make it just for the evening.'

She laughed. 'Did you say I bossed my boss? I don't even get asked will I come, just told I'm going.'

'Will you come, then?'

'Yes, I just love Elspeth and Dougal.'

'Thank you very much. You've as odd a way of accepting as I apparently had of asking. You'll come because you love Elspeth and Dougal, not because you'd enjoy *my* company!'

She pulled a saucy face at him. 'Well, possibly that too, but as I don't feel your ego needs any bolstering, I didn't bother saying so. Come on, I like to be back at the house for the children, and anyway, I've promised them they can teach me to ride a donkey after school.'

Barnabas followed her down, but on the bridge restrained her, a hand on her arm. 'What did you mean, my ego doesn't need bolstering up? That's the sort of thing said to a chap who was conceited. Do I give that impression? Is it an employer complex?'

She looked up, astonished, 'Good heavens, no, not with you.'

'Good, because Dad was so determined I shouldn't get bigheaded, that when I completed my studies in botany and joined the firm, he sent me off to a Christchurch store for a year and told the owner I was to have no concessions at all. I'd hate to think I developed it through the years. Are you sure you didn't mean that? I can take it.'

She gave him another saucy look. 'Not in the least . . . it was everything of the most personal . . . so you'll probably not like it any better . . . I meant that when a gorgeous blonde like Melisande was so evidently jealous to find you working with a former secretary in what almost looked like a love-nest, you ought to think yourself no end of a guy.'

He lifted a hand to smack her and she fled, with him in hot pursuit, not stopping till they reached the front where an amazed Rosina, watering the fuchsia baskets on the porch, brought them to a halt by saying, 'What on earth are you two up to?'

Barnabas reached Priscilla, caught her with one hand, swung her round and shook her, not gently. Rosina stared.

Barnabas said, 'She's getting above herself. I've no scruples about wielding a good old masculine fist when this sort of thing happens. She can think herself lucky you were there.' He was laughing helplessly at the look on his aunt's face.

He said to Priscilla, 'It's bad enough having Rosina try to manage my life without you setting in on an analytical survey. By the time the two of you have finished with me and my love-life, I'll have no ego left. I can scarcely recognise myself. Rosina, you're coming down to the donkey meadow with us too. I want you to try to recall all the incidents possible that were concerned with Jesmond Dene's donkeys.

'Wasn't there some tale about them eating into a haystack and it caving in on one called Jerusha, and you diving to the rescue and Manuel just getting the two of you out in the nick of time? Sounds like Sweet Alicia, doesn't it? Even if she's kith, not kin, she still could be said to take after you.'

Priscilla said, 'I love Alicia so much it hurts. It's far from all joy, but I wouldn't have it otherwise. I'd love to be round when she grows up. By then she'll be more discriminating and not fall for all the hard-luck stories, but she'll be a power for good. She'll make a lot of mistakes by leaping before she looks, but she'll bring such warmth of heart to all her endeavours that the world will be lovelier just because she was in it. I find myself dreading certain things for her, like marrying for pity instead of love, because her heart is bigger than her body, or being disillusioned because she expects too much from people.'

She expected something derisive from Barnabas, so was most surprised when he said, 'But even if she did, marry for pity, I mean, she'd make a fine thing out of it. You mean if she went in for nursing and married a paraplegic or something? But some girls have married paraplegics for love, anyway.

'She probably will know disillusionment, that's the price she'll pay for high ideals, but what's the betting that with some she'll get the high response because it's what she expects of them? Don't they say hero-worship begets heroes? I behave better myself when Alicia says, "But you wouldn't do a mean thing like that, would you, Uncle Barnabas?" I just dare not let her down. Oh, keep and save us, here they are. Thank goodness Nat and Tim are just nice ordinary uncomplicated schoolboys not given to fighting other people's battles like their sister.'

The nice ordinary schoolboys came into view first, on their cycles, each bearing the signs of conflict. The sleeve was half torn out of Tim's shirt, his knees were gravel-pitted and bloody, and Nat was wearing what was surely an incipient black eye, had a cut forehead, swollen lips and an unmistakable air of triumph.

Alicia, in a determined effort to tell the tale first, shot on her bike between the two boys with an inch to spare either side, Priscilla was sure, and to her delight Barnabas had to spring madly out of her path. She braked with such force it was a wonder she wasn't thrown over the handlebars and flung herself on Barnabas. 'Oh, I do wish you'd been there! It was absolutely beaut. Tim and Nat were magnificent. You should've seen Murdoch Fraserby's nose bleed. Nat gave him a terrific punch, with his left hand too, and that sent him flying off Timothy and he was able to scramble up. That great bully had leapt on little Johnny Pascoe from the school wall. Tim had rushed to his aid, but was having a hard time of it till Nat arrived.'

Barnabas took hold of Alicia, surveyed her, said, 'And then you pitched in.'

Alicia looked staggered. 'How did you know? I said the boys weren't to tell you, in case I got into trouble.'

Her courtesy uncle grinned. 'Your frock is absolutely spattered with blood ... Fraserby's blood, I sincerely hope, and you're covered in dust. It looks to me as if you were flung into the dust but rose to fight another day.'

'She rose to fight there and then,' said Nat, grinning. 'I had to haul her off him finally. She didn't know when to stop.' He looked regretful. 'I had to make myself stop too —wouldn't have been fair otherwise. Even a chap his size couldn't take the three of us on. He'd had enough, any-way.'

'Well, everybody wash your face, get into jeans and have a snack. Then it's us for the donkey meadow. We're all going.'

Alicia said, 'Just as well Nerolie wasn't with us today. Her mother's taken her into Dunedin for shoes. She sees enough violence in her own home, it upsets her. It doesn't upset me. Well, it does sort of, but it's kind of a change, if you know what I mean.'

'I'm not sure what you mean by violence, Alicia,' said Barnabas. 'What do you think it consists of ... does the father drink, or is it just a case of a kid getting spanked for misdeeds and exaggerating?'

Alicia shook her head—reluctantly, they noticed. 'No, he doesn't drink. But they're cruel to her in lots of ways. She says they don't get on together, so they take it out on her. Especially her mother. Of course her mother never wanted her and never got used to having a youngster round the house making it untidy.'

Priscilla said doubtfully, 'She doesn't look neglected. She's exquisitely dressed.'

'That's their pride. Besides, if she looked like you said . . . neglected, someone would report it, Nerolie said. Sneaky, isn't it?'

'But only if that's true,' said Barnabas practically. 'Some kids do tell whoppers, you know, Sweet Alice. They like to be dramatic. It makes them feel important. What's the mother like when you go there?'

'Sugary. It can't be for real. She's just like any mother then. That's the cunning of it.'

'Well, off with you now. Get changed, then we're for the donkey-riding.' He added to Priscilla when they'd gone, 'Don't look so distressed. This sort of thing's happened before with Alicia. She's so obviously a sucker, she's always the recipient of sob-stories. Zillah once realised that Alicia was woefully short of pocket-money when it came to the boys' birthdays, and accused her of spending more than was allowed on sweets. Alicia answered virtuously, yes, she was, but not for herself. That there was a little girl at school who had never as much as had a bar of chocolate in her life, so she was giving her a treat. It turned out the child was overweight and they'd been trying to diet her and were wondering why they hadn't succeeded.'

Priscilla felt much lighter-hearted. 'You're good for me. I tend to take things too seriously, even though I'm a giggler at times when I shouldn't be. I don't even understand myself sometimes. For a born optimist in most things, when it comes to other people's lives I'm always sure they're suffering deeply, and I agonise for them.'

Rosina had followed the children in, so they were alone.

Barnabas looked at her, said, seriously, 'I'm glad you realise that, Priscilla. I've been working that out myself. It's very endearing, but possibly painful for you, and—forgive me—a little weakening for the people you care about. I don't want to sound as if I'm running an advice column, but that's how it all started with Clarice and Roger, wasn't it?'

It was most engaging the way her smile started so slowly, the corners of her mouth beginning to lift, then suddenly her whole face lighting up. She had no idea how attractive it was.

'I've got to admit that. Since that talk with Roger I've seen myself in a new light. I wasn't really good for Clarice so she leaned on me. But when she married again I ought to have cut adrift and left them to themselves. Well, I did try, but Clarice begged me not to. If I'm being honest, I'd admit I rather liked the feeling of being necessary to someone. I thought Roger was such a brick and deserved some help. I felt my being there—or near—helped him adjust, let them have evenings out like any other couple in the first year of marriage. But——'

Barnabas had possessed himself of her hands. 'That's big of you, Priscilla. I like that. Don't go back on it, will you? Any time your feeling for—your feeling of being sorry for Roger sweeps over you, be strong. Be strong for his sake. A marriage is at stake. I know Clarice is a weak character and at present she's a bit sore with you for upping and offing, but a tree doesn't need a stake all its life. Comes a time when it deepens its roots and can stand up to all the winds that blow. So, even if at times you long to—to be kind to Roger—curb the impulse. It isn't wise.'

Her almond-shaped brown eyes lit up. 'That's very nicely put. I don't feel censured for having been so indulgent towards my own inclination for coddling people a bit. Neither have you made me feel a martyr that I was tied to my sister so long. Very few people would be discriminating.' She suddenly looked thoughtful. 'Did I say anything to you about Clarice being sore? I don't remember.'

The blue eyes were watchful instantly, as if he wanted to gauge by her expression her possible reaction to his answer. 'This seems to be the moment for confidences. Without offence being taken. I went out to see your sister.'

Surprise, not indignation, flashed over her features. 'I dare not resent that.' She grinned. 'But why?'

He seemed to be seeking words. She was still smiling. 'I get it. When you found me here, knew I'd deceived you, you felt you must see my background for your aunt's sake. Fair enough.'

Again he hesitated, then said, 'I expect that was it.'

'And what did you find, Barnabas? There's only one thing that would worry me. If you gave Clarice any hint that Roger and I had——'

He came in quickly. 'I certainly didn't. Didn't hint I'd ever met him. When Roger came in, I managed to say something fairly loudly as he entered on the lines of: "Oh, is this your husband now?" and he picked up his cue quickly and we met as strangers. I'd just dropped in with some flowers, gave them to Clarice and said I thought I should meet the family of the girl who was looking after my aunt and to say how glad I was that you could, that I was sure you missed them all, but it had relieved me of much anxiety, so much so that I was willing to forgo your valuable help in the office.

'Clarice moaned a little about missing you, said it wasn't so easy now to go away with Roger . . . that was the worst of being married to a man who had to travel a lot in his job and so on. But he's not always on the road, is he?'

'No, just occasionally, and Clarice did overdo a bit, going with him. Roger found it a bit hampering. She was inclined to want him to show her round each place, when his time wasn't his own, but they'll work it out.' She smiled at him again. 'I thought I'd worry over them dreadfully, feel guilty if Clarice couldn't quite cope, or got ill, but I'm discovering things about myself I didn't know. Like Zillah will be doing, finding out that the hub of the universe goes with you wherever you go or whoever you leave behind. I've had other things on my mind ever since I came out here and with Nat, Tim and Sweet Alice to look after, I've had no time to worry.'

'Good show . . . ah, here they are, off we go!'

They had a hilarious two hours, finishing up with a romp

in the hay, then getting into the bathing suits Barnabas had ordered them to bring, and bathing in a willow-cool river pool where the Fairmead Water wound down from its source in the Maungatuas. Priscilla was an excellent swimmer and looked like a dryad in a leaf-green bikini. Rosina, the romantic, said so, making them all laugh.

'And she doesn't mind getting her hair wet,' added Barnabas. 'It spoils your fun to be out with a girl who just frisks on the edge and thinks sunbathing on a rock is a substitute for diving into the depths. Priscilla, your wet hair as you come up looks just like a sea-leopard's head.'

She burst out laughing, dashing water out of her eyes. 'What a compliment . . . you mean a drowned rat!'

'Well, I know a very handsome pair of water-rats live in a hole in the bank of a creek that feeds into this. They're a sort of sleek acorn-brown with a dash of tawny colour, just like your hair, and long, beautiful whiskers.'

'And with that, I can't compete,' mourned Priscilla, feeling each side of her mouth. 'Sea-leopards, acorns, rats . . . some girls get compared to spun gold, newly-minted copper, ebony and platinum when it comes to their hair. All the precious symbols.'

He scooped up a handful of water, flung it at her, said, 'But what do precious metals mean to me? Those are the things I like to draw . . . water-rats, acorns, sea-creatures . . . you can't draw spun gold.'

Priscilla turned on her back, floating, looking up at the sky. Barnabas joined her, his shoulder touching hers. Rosina and the children were building a dam of river-stones across a little backwater made by half-submerged willow roots. So they were in a world of their own, bounded by cool, pure water beneath them, rimmed by a circle of blue sky above, that was fringed with the tops of the green willow fronds of the high branches.

As one they turned and looked at each other, one of those long friendship-forging looks that leap time and depth of feeling. Then when it might have been embarrassing to hold that look longer he said, 'Could you work this into your script, Priscilla? This willow-fringed pool, sky and leaves making two circles, one a reflection, and the little Ambrosina kneeling on the bank, gazing down into the depth and thinking the long, long thoughts of childhood?'

The slow smile dawned, then the following eagerness and certainty flashing in the brown depths. 'Oh, I could, I could. Barnabas, I must make for the bank. I've my jotter-book in my pinny-pocket. I always have to get a flash of inspiration like that down pronto or it fades, or gets overlaid with other ones.'

He swam across with her, helped her clamber up, said ruefully, 'Now I've spoiled our idyll, our own idyll. Could anything have been more perfect than that bathe today, in this setting?'

She laughed, 'No, but on paper, in your sketch, and in the words I'll weave round it, it will always be ours.'

'And every time we see it, even when we're old and grey, we'll recapture that.'

She bent over her discarded clothes, fished out the notebook, deep in the capacious pocket of her artist's smock, hid her flushed face from him. It was just the artist in him that made him speak like that, not the man. Don't be foolish, Priscilla. Don't hope, then you won't be disappointed. But oh, if only Melisande hadn't been so firmly entrenched in Barnabas Lockhart's life since so long ago!

Rosina couldn't hide her pleasure at Priscilla having a night out. Priscilla knew that some of this was because she much preferred to see her nephew out with someone she found a kindred spirit herself, rather than the superficial Melisande, and she wished Rosina wouldn't be so transparent.

She flicked Rosina's cheek with a finger, said, 'You're so scared that I'll sweep too clean like the new broom, and refuse to be torn away from Jesmond Dene, that you're insisting on your companion having a night off. I've not wanted it till now. This has been like a holiday. Fair-acre

Valley is so beautiful, with its hills and dells, its English trees and its native bush gullies, that I've no desire to go into the city for any entertainments, especially with that darling chalet in the larch wood, like something out of a Swiss fairytale. The world of business seems a million miles away.'

Barnabas laughed, 'I was taken to task for doubtful compliments today, but you've dropped a real clanger. *I* was part of that world of business, remember?'

She nodded, one dimple cleaving her smooth brown cheek. 'In fact, you *were* the business. But you have a dual nature. One is the big business tycoon, the other is the artist, about to create a world of delight for children and adults alike.'

'Well, you said you were a born optimist ... I'd say a super-optimist. To anticipate a success like that for us. You make me sound a schizophrenic. You know, the old split personality thingamy.'

'No, just a many-faceted personality.'

'That sounds much better. Goodness, I *do* like you better away from the office. You were so severe I was almost scared of you. It was a relief to go out with someone as hellbent on enjoyment as the fair Melisande, but now I don't pay her wages, Priscilla Marchant is almost human.'

Alicia said, in shocked tones, 'Uncle Barnabas, you *can't* mean you didn't like her?'

Fortunately he was saved a reply by Nat who said, 'Ninny ... if he hadn't liked her very much he wouldn't have cared and he certainly wouldn't have told her now.'

'Now, there's someone who knows his onions,' said Barnabas admiringly.

Alicia thought differently. 'I don't think I know what Nat means.'

Barnabas swung her up. 'Honey, he just means that with people we really like we can be very natural. Now, we have time for one game of Ludo before Priscilla and I go out. But she can't play, she has to make herself beautiful. And mind, you haven't got to care if you lose.'

As Priscilla came down the stairs Rosina turned, said, 'I've never seen you in blue before ... some brown girls don't suit blue, but you've that lovely colour, and the white collar and cuffs against your tanned skin are perfect. Blue as azure as the sky with cloud-white spots ... perfection!'

'Doesn't your aunt marry off words delightfully?' Priscilla said to Barnabas. 'But watch what you say, Ambrosina Claremont, it's likely to be taken down and published about you, between your nephew and your companion. My brother Andrew sent me this dress from Paris. Very courageous of him because for once he didn't have his wife with him. It was absolutely perfect as regards fit.'

He looked at her shoes. 'I'd intended asking if you felt like walking, but with shoes like that, we'll take the car.'

Priscilla turned immediately. 'I'll change them. I wouldn't put these bits of frivolity against a ramble in the summer dusk for anything.' Before he could protest she was running upstairs and came down again in another pair of white shoes, but with lower heels.

Rosina and the children waved them goodbye from the steps, and watched them down the drive till the bend hid them from sight. Barnabas stopped, put his hand under a scarlet, sweet scented Etoile de Holland rose, fully blown, to savour its perfume, only to have it scatter every petal on the ground. 'The last rose of summer ...' he quoted.

'But not left blooming alone,' countered Priscilla. She waved a hand at the myriad roses still in bud and bloom, promise of a bonus of summer for the first month of the Southern Hemisphere autumn, March. But so often then, if the South Pole below them decided it was time, winds with icy edges would steal up to Southland and Otago, and begin the colourful alchemy of the fall.

'Summer always lingers in Rosina's garden,' said her nephew, 'not because of all this twaddle talked about green fingers and magic, which really boils down to sweating hours and aching backs, but because she and Manuel created shelter-belts of trees and brushwood fences, little brick walls and low hedges to protect their loved bushes from the malicious south, and it worked.'

'How true. It makes me think of Goldsmith's village of Auburn . . . do you get me?'

He thought for a moment. 'Oh, yes . . . "Where smiling spring her earliest visit paid and long-departing Summer still delayed." '

'Oh, Barnabas, I'm so glad you gave that version. I learned it that way at school, but in a book I have it gives it as: ". . . and parting Summer's lingering blooms delayed," and I like your version better.'

Such a little thing, but it all added up to joy and kindredness . . . his ability to quote poetry. He'd done it earlier when they were working on the book. It was something Priscilla still missed her father for. And tonight, at the Manse, there would probably be more of it. Already one star had peeped out over Liberty Hill. What a night!

CHAPTER SEVEN

BARNABAS said, 'Some day I'll take you up there, Priscilla. It's beautiful by day or by night. You look right across, south of Saddle Hill, to the sea. You can see the lights in the clusters of cottages here and there, and once in a while those of a ship moving out on the vastness of the Pacific, or a big plane zooming up from the South Pole, with its red and green lights. Ever thought you'd like to take one of those tourist trips over Antarctica they're running from Christchurch now?'

She shook her head decidedly. 'No. It would be fantastic, of course, but it isn't quite my scene. I stay on earth in my dreams.'

He was silent for a moment. 'What a delightful sentence! We must repeat that to Elspeth. She'd love it. Can you make it more specific? What sort of dreams?'

She turned an astonished face to him. 'Do you know, I don't quite know. I've always been dreamy. But if it's a question of defining what I most long for, I just don't know.' (Apart from longing for you, her heart said to her mind.)

'I can tell you,' said Barnabas boldly.

More astonishment. Again she turned to him and this time stopped dead. 'How could you possibly know?'

'You let me take your published stories for children to read at home, so I could get the trend of your creative thought as you said in your precisely quaint way. It's all there, Priscilla. All your dreams are woven round homes and gardens. Family homes where children are loved and wanted; where they know security and fun, and grow up among donkeys and hens and chickens, have puppies and kittens, and wake up to see trees waving outside windows

114

and smell all the scents of the garden and newmown hay and pine-groves. Am I not right?'

She recognised it and admitted it. Of a sudden, standing there in the country road, with the village houses just round the next bend, she felt afraid of the future, of herself . . . and the strange thing was that she was afraid because she knew he was drawn to her in spite of his distrust over the incident of the letter, so there were rocks ahead. Oh, Barnabas, Barnabas, if only there hadn't been Melisande in your life! But I'm not the type to take a man away from another woman . . . although until now I've never thought of myself as being able to do it. But I could, with Barnabas, if I encouraged him, because we are so kindred. But I couldn't do that to Melisande. It seems as if she tried life without him once and came back to him, and even if they aren't engaged, they're as near as doesn't matter.

She became aware that he was watching her closely, smiling a little, and in no hurry to move. She said, 'If anyone comes round the corner and sees us like this, having an obviously serious conversation stock-still in the middle of the road, they'll think we're nutty. Let's go on.'

He chuckled. 'Yes, decidedly odd. Oh, the things we have to do, or not do, because it would look odd to someone we don't care two hoots about.'

She must get away from the too-personal. 'Tell me about Dougal and Elspeth. How did they meet, and where?'

'I'm not clear on all the details, but in Christchurch I think. Elspeth had been down here and bought a cottage, intending to give up her job as an advertising clerk with a firm like ours. She bought the Crooked House, behind the Manse, where her uncle and Dougal's uncle live now. When manse life gets too much for her, or she has a deadline, like returning proofs, she retires to the Crooked House when the children are at school. I've a vague idea Dougal called on her about the sale of the property to her.'

'They're such a lovely couple, you can only imagine the course of true love ran smoothly for them. I hope it did. The way Elspeth regards Dougal's niece and nephew just as she does her own two warms the heart.'

Barnabas had her cool bare elbow cupped in his hand, helping her where the path was rough. She was vividly aware of his touch. He guffawed, 'Get Elspeth to tell you some time. Only she could do full justice to it. Remember we just passed that path up to the top of Liberty Hill? Well, Dougal, a supposedly sober member of the cloth, fell in love at first sight, and the first Sunday she was here proposed to her up there after the evening service. But it took him months to win her. She thought she was no wife for a minister.'

'Elspeth? Oh, you're having me on. She's ideal.'

'Of course. Well, it's common knowledge, so I break no confidences—I'll tell you some time, but nobody should look at what they think is an ideal pair and imagine that *their* path was strewn with roses.'

'No, it's silly. Sometimes you look at people who appear so carefree, who seem to lack for nothing, feel they're fortune's darlings, and you find out that a horrible anxiety is gnawing at them. Barnabas, we're getting too profound, let's snap out of it.'

Nobody would have dreamed Elspeth and Dougal had had a day so varied, they were so gay. It had been tragic and hilarious, annoying and uplifting. They'd run the gamut of many emotions. A funeral, a wedding, sick visiting squeezed in somehow, and some petty complaints over the phone that Elspeth had shielded Dougal from because he was needed more by folk in dire trouble and she couldn't let small-minded people like these filch his time and energies from those others who were the salt of the earth, time that was theirs by right.

Dougal referred to that briefly, said, 'Elspeth is just coming. I'm glad you're here. She needs a little light relief. She always weeps with those who weep, and rejoices with those who rejoice, but going straight from the funeral of that loved child, to enter into the spirit of the wedding, took a lot out of her. The children, all four of them, are spending the night at the Crooked House with the uncles, who've got a new and complicated dice game for them. Better Ben and Timothy should teach them than us. We invariably get interrupted and it's so frustrating for the young even if, in theory, it teaches them others must come first.'

The Manse drawing-room was huge, with good but shabby furniture, and, as Dougal painted in oils, some charming New Zealand scenes, mostly of the Lake County, hung on the walls. Everywhere, of course, were books. Double glass doors at the far end were open on to a big loggia with garden furniture scattered round, and there they sat till it was moonrise, and the absence of strong light made it easier to exchange views on shoes and ships and sealing-wax and cabbages and kings.

When they came inside, Priscilla was surprised when Barnabas began to speak freely of their joint venture. He grinned. 'Priscilla didn't know I was going to bring this up. I think the fact that you've published nearly a dozen novels, Elspeth, makes her feel very much a beginner. But I'd like you and Dougal to visit us at the chalet when we're working there, some day, because you two would certainly be qualified to criticise.'

Elspeth's green eyes, intensified by the emerald and black frock she was wearing, sparkled. 'Barnabas, does this mean that at last you're using your talent? You've been far too conscientious about serving your employees and your father . . . he's a darling and immensely appreciative about you carrying on, but it could eat up all your time and I don't like it. Priscilla, I hope you know that as far as this man's concerned, you're a godsend. It was very noble of you to let your aunt filch your secretary from you, Barnabas, but I think that now you're reaping more bountifullly than you sowed.'

Priscilla tried not to catch Barnabas's eye, but was too late. She saw his mouth beginning to crumble, felt her own going and they gave way to uncontrollable mirth, to the amazement of Elspeth and Dougal, even though the laughter was so irresistible they joined in. Priscilla knew alarm. Barnabas was in an expansive mood and could reveal the whole set-up, and she wouldn't come out of it in too good a light.

It was reassuring that he lulled her fears immediately. He winked at Priscilla, said, 'Can't tell you all, because it's too involved, but when she took on Rosina she'd no idea she *was* my aunt. She'd always heard me referred to as Mr Peter. Well, you know how I always try to restrain my volatile aunt, and how we have each other on, so she refers to me as the horrible Barnabas? Well, I'd got her to deliver by hand those questionnaires for the Horticultural Society, plus a letter for my aunt—and that was the night, of course, when you discovered them falling out of the tree, Dougal. Priscilla was just starting her holidays, had made up her mind to give up her job to do more writing, impulsively decided to give Rosina a hand with the children ... then I went out to see my aunt, mad as a meat-axe with her because she already had the children installed, and I found that this paragon my aunt had extolled to me as her new companion was none other than my secretary! She'd sent me her notice, with her Dunedin address on it, you see. We both blew up!'

'I can understand this,' said Elspeth, giggling at the thought of such a confrontation, 'because it's just what I did. I gave up a job north to live in a shabby little cottage to write. And instead,' she gave Dougal a saucy look, 'I landed myself into housekeeping for the Manse, plus Dougal's niece and nephew and his uncle. We must both be softies, Priscilla. Aren't they lucky to get us?'

'Er—well——' Priscilla stammered, hot-cheeked and glad the wall-lights were low. 'It isn't exactly the same. Barnabas and I are just business partners.' She recovered a little and said cheekily, 'At least I've not got the chore of cooking for him.'

Mercifully Barnabas let it pass. The evening sped on wings. They talked little on the way home. A contentment such as Priscilla had never known before descended upon her. She knew it for a transient thing, but certainly a night to remember. She was glad of his hand under her elbow again, but when they entered the dark tunnel of tree-backed fuchsia drive, because the moon that had been playing hide-and-seek for some time with massing clouds, disappeared completely, he slipped his hand further along her forearm and engulfed hers. Oh, how odd, in a draper, to feel hard callouses in his palm. She said so, added, 'I didn't know for so long that you were also a part-time farmer, yet you have the fingers of the true artist.'

He said nothing, at first. She waited. She could just see the outline of his face with its strong jaw and high cheekbones faintly, because they were now on the fringe of light cast by the one lamp Rosina had left on the porch.

His fingers tightened over hers as he looked down on her. 'You've done more for my ego than anyone else has, bar Mother. I've plodded for years trying to be the successful heir to a family concern. I felt I was born to the responsibility of that. Oh, dear, don't I sound priggish?'

She shook him with her free hand. 'Don't be ridiculous. We don't always have to depreciate these things. You wouldn't say that to everyone, but we've talked pretty deeply this night by ourselves and with the MacNabs. Go on, Peter Barnabas Lockhart.'

'But this task, Priscilla, that we're doing together, will satisfy something in me that was getting stifled. I won't neglect the other. I owe that to scores of people who make their livelihood at Lockhart's, in fact I'll probably do a better job on that because I won't feel so frustrated, but just as you said that living here and being able to get on with your writing more had opened up a new world for you, so with me, now. And in the same place.'

She felt so filled with happiness for him she couldn't speak.

He continued. 'Take Melisande, for instance. She's always told me I've no ambition because I don't make the most of my chances, that in a position like mine I could travel more. I have to at times, but I always head for home when business trips are over. She says I have chances I should seize, that certain contacts and deals could double the business. I don't crave that. I'd like to think that even in these days, there's still room for family firms, that I'll be able always to put a name to every face behind the counters.' He laughed. 'I wonder what sort of an ambition she'd think this . . . to become an illustrator of books for children. Ready cash and big deals are what appeal more to Melisande.'

Priscilla had to ask it. 'When she gets to know, as she's bound to eventually, will you allow it to affect you?'

'How?'

'Will you let it deter you?'

'Do you think I'd allow it to?'

'I'd hope not. Not purely because it's so wonderful for me to have an illustrator of your calibre at hand but because——'

'Go on. Because——?'

'Because it would be hiding a talent in the ground, and the Bible has some harsh words to say on that subject.'

'Well, that's one reason and a good one. But I hoped it might be something different, something more personal to me.'

She hesitated, then said, 'My first and foremost reason is because I want this thing for *you*. For you to fulfil what must have been the early promise of your schoolboy days.'

He uttered a sound she thought she could interpret as nothing but satisfaction. Then he said, 'Thank you. I hoped for that.'

She hesitated again, then said, 'Barnabas, I hope you don't think I'm trying to decry Melisande. It's just I feel you owe it to your gift to cultivate it. It might happen she doesn't realise how much it means to you or what pleasure it could bring to generations of children.'

'I won't think that. It isn't Melisande's fault—that she has limitations, I mean. She was brought up to value everything in terms of monetary value. It's criminal to bring children up on a yardstick like that. Melisande, fortunately, struck a bad patch. That may sound odd . . . but it was good for her. Suddenly her life seemed a bit meaningless, and she took up this technical job at the hospital, and it's brought her into contact with so many cases of people living in what she'd term poor circumstances, and even suffering quite badly, yet still enjoying life and putting up a battle to retain it, that her sense of values is shifting. But it still doesn't mean I want to tell her about this—yet. Does that make sense?'

'It does. I think it's wise. Oh, Barnabas, I feel that at long last, with your help, I'm going to be able to break through into that other world I've longed to enter for years . . . the magic of seeing one's thoughts and dreams in print on a page embellished with drawings that express it perfectly. Anything that happened before Christmas—like living in a flat and working as a secretary—seems a million light-years away. I go cold at the thought that if you hadn't asked me to deliver those notices in Fair-acre Valley I might have missed all this.'

He smiled down on her. 'So do I.'

He meant, of course, that he might have missed his chance of doing what he most wanted to do, but how sweet if he had meant anything else.

They weren't far from where he'd left his car in front of the steps. Priscilla said, 'We mustn't linger any longer. You've got to go beyond Dunedin to Tyne Hill. It's late. We'll have so much time ahead of us to discuss our work. You must go.'

He laughed, 'Yes, but first this . . . but stay in the shadows for it, Priscilla. I'd not put it past Rosina, bless her romantic heart, to be watching out of her window and goodness knows how much she'd read into it.'

He brought his mouth down on hers, gathered her closer. There was sheer magic in it for Priscilla. She didn't know what there was in it for Barnabas Lockhart. Possibly just the pleasure of the moment. That last remark of his had been revealing. It was a qualifying statement, perhaps a slight warning not to take him too seriously.

As he released her she said lightly, 'Perhaps we can be excused for this. We're still on the crest of feeling our work can enhance each other's, that is if I can produce work worthy of their illustrations. We've let this setting go to our heads. It's a bit much, isn't it? ... Old-world garden, moonlight and roses. Don't let's get carried away, Barnabas, ours is a working partnership. Goodnight.'

There was immediately a hint of restraint, of withdrawal in the way he echoed her goodnight. He got into the car, drove away.

Priscilla was glad Rosina didn't call out. She wanted no ordinary conversation to overlay the enchantment of this evening. She didn't want anyone, even as dear as Rosina, to guess, by the look of her, that she'd just been kissed. She felt it would be mirrored in her eyes, like candles lit.

Day succeeded lovely day. March came in with burnished harvest fields and at the top of Liberty Hill, not so sheltered as in the dene below, the poplar leaves were now tipped with gold and the rowans were turning russet. In Rosina's garden rows of nerines were marching in ranks along the borders, pink and white and coral dusted with gold powder. Petunias and marigolds, geraniums and stocks vied with each other to produce the most vivid hues, pansies patterned the crevices with wise little faces of purple and brown, but the dahlias began to droop, and the buds on the chrysanthemums waxed fat.

Even the vegetable garden had its own beauty as tasselly heads of corn grew tall and straight, tomatoes reddened on the vines on the back fence, lettuces were kept going by constant watering, and added their own pattern with green rosettes. Priscilla felt she saw everything through an artist's eye because Barnabas pointed out these things. She realised now how it was that in a staff emergency he could substitute for a window-dresser. In the old orchard the children knew nectar-sweet playtime hours as they ate greengages straight from the trees, late plums, nectarines, apples.

That child Nerolie had the most enormous appetite which made Priscilla wonder at times if she did have enough to eat, but she was highly-strung and whipcord-lean, so perhaps she just burned up her intake in nervous energy.

The days were full, house-cleaning, gardening, washing and mending and baking, yet there was always the blessing of those hours Barnabas could spend away from the shop. Virginia creeper, turning multi-coloured in autumn splendour, peeped in at the little casements in the chalet, and through them they could see old Fergus MacKinnon cutting his field of red clover. There had been MacKinnons on that farm for a hundred and thirty years, ever since the Church of Scotland settlement had reached Otago.

'Perhaps there's been red clover in that field since that time,' said Barnabas, watching him. 'Great ones for tradition, the MacKinnons. Never think he was in his eighties, would you? Shall we have red clover in our book, Priscilla? Little Ambrosina could be picking it.' His pencil was roughly sketching in the haystack and the oat-stacks. 'Am I right in imagining that these days there are a few more working horses about than of old? Might be a good thing if the shortage and price of oil has brought that about.

'Odd how these days I see adventures for Ambrosina wherever I go. I'm obsessed by that child. But isn't it fascinating to know so much material is to hand? Sometimes, as now, it's seeing Fergus at his red clover, but more often it's your pile of script. That lot I took home two nights ago had me laughing out loud. I was reading it in bed at one in the morning, and Mrs Forsythe got up to find out what on earth was going on. I'd clean forgotten what time it was. Your description of Elspeth's fowlyard was irresistible. A motley lot, Black Orpingtons, Silver Wyandottes, Australorps and White Leghorns, bantams and strutting cocks, and the pickle Ambrosina got into with them all. I have to keep remembering Elspeth is called Morag in this.'

'I just love Elspeth,' said Priscilla. 'I chuckle every time I imagine—or try to—thinking she wasn't good enough for a minister's wife. She told me all about it the other day.'

Barnabas nodded. 'Dougal didn't care tuppence, said to me once he could read Elspeth's worth. That she was how his Uncle Timothy defined her, steel-true, blade-straight. But even when he thought there must be something unorthodox in her past, he loved her just the same.'

'That's as any woman would want it. In spite of——'

'In spite of what?'

'In spite of one's imperfections, I suppose. In spite of being mistrusted.'

He looked at her sharply and she knew her colour rose. She said, 'That applies not in just man-woman situations, Barnabas, but in friendships too. Mistrust can undermine them.'

He said, 'There's something in your voice makes this important. Priscilla, I admit I was sore when you pretended you were in Christchurch and thinking of settling there. I was flaming mad in fact. But since I've got to know you more, I feel you had some very good reason and I want you to know that though at times, naturally, I still wonder, I now completely trust you. I couldn't see you with Rosina, with the children, working for a much smaller salary, and still distrust you.'

He was rewarded with the slow wide smile, the sudden light in the eyes. 'Thank you, Barnabas. Being trusted on intuition is much nicer than on explanation. If I could turn time back I'd act differently. I should have just written saying I'd changed my mind about holidaying up north, that I'd been asked to help an elderly woman with the care of some children and it appealed, so I wanted to resign. Her name and address would have appeared, you'd have rung me up, said of all the coincidences, she was your aunt.' She laughed, added, 'Mind you, you'd have tried to dissuade me, wouldn't you? Because you didn't want Rosina encouraged to take them. But once we'd got that ironed out, there'd have been no distrust.'

'Fair enough. Will you tell me some day what it was all about?'

She thought that over, aware he was watching her closely. 'Well, if ever I *could* speak frankly about it, yes, I'd be glad to tell you.' A smile curved her lips. She was thinking that the only circumstances in which she could tell Barnabas the truth was if he came to care for her, and it was an extremely remote chance. Just wishful thinking. Because there was Melisande, and Barnabas had hinted tactfully the other night that he hadn't wanted Rosina to read too much into their seemingly intimate conversations in an old-world garden.

He frowned. Priscilla had a wistful air, as if she hankered after some impossible dream. He said roughly, 'Well, let's get on with the job in hand. Trouble is that in creative work like this, especially children's stuff which is necessarily nostalgic, one tends to get sentimental.'

Stung, Priscilla said, 'I think you were the one who digressed, brought in the personal note. I'd be very happy to keep this whole thing to strictly business.'

Instantly he said, fleetingly touching her hand as it lay on the table between them, 'Don't, Priscilla. I mean, don't take offence with me. I'm a moody beggar at the moment. I—I hardly understand myself. I've got——'

Her eyes went watchful. 'You've got——?'

'I've got all sorts of inner conflicts. There are some emotions I'm battling with for the first time in my life, so bear with me.'

Her creamy lids dropped down over the almond eyes, so he couldn't read her expression. He couldn't possibly know how she longed to beg him to tell her all about it.

But no, she mustn't. Instead she said, 'Barnabas, I've been the same. This last year has been all inner conflicts. But time seems to be taking care of a lot of things for me. Is this something that time may resolve for you?'

He was frowning down on his doodling pencil. 'Could be. It's so tied up with other people. I'm not by nature patient. But though my desire is to hammer this thing out without delay, all my instincts tell me it would be too precipitate . . . unkind to boot.'

'I can't even pretend to guess at it, but if your instinct urges you to wait, I'd trust to it if I were you.'

His smile was wry. 'I was afraid of that advice. But everything selfish in me wishes you'd said why not go ahead.'

'Oh, Barnabas, you scare me! I'm working in the dark. I ought not to have ventured a single word—it was foolish in the extreme. Forget it. Trust your own judgment.'

He nodded. 'I will. I oughtn't to have mentioned it. Back to little Ambrosina. To her world of donkeys and hedgehogs and red clover and her flair for adventure. The more we work on it the more I'm convinced you've got a winner, Priscilla.'

'*We've* got a winner.'

He conceded that. 'Right. How odd things turn out! I was so against Rosina having the oversight of the Darfield children, yet but for that, I'd never have had this dropped into my lap. You'd have gone north for your holiday and looked for a job up there. What quirks Fate has in store for us at times!'

Priscilla chuckled. 'I didn't think much of Fate the day you stepped out of the car and I thought it much worse than if a pompous, portly and prosperous Barnabas had appeared. I was prepared to meet a curmudgeon of a chap who couldn't stand children. I felt Rosina so obviously loved them and loved Zillah that it was a natural choice. I was prepared to do battle with this bossy nephew, but once we simmered down, I was glad it was you.'

'Why? The situation was the same.'

She coloured a little. 'Having worked with you a year I did know, under my surface antagonism, that your motives could be only of the highest, concern for Rosina.'

Barnabas looked comically surprised. 'Yes, you're definitely good for the old ego. You know my exasperation with Zillah for going off and leaving her children was part of this feeling I have—what is it?—Exasperation when generous-hearted, stronger characters let weaker ones lean on them and therefore become weaker still. Rosina has always coped, a tiny, indomitable little thing. I felt that at her age she'd earned a respite. I felt disappointed in Zillah. I thought she'd never have left her children like this.'

Priscilla made up her mind. 'Barnabas, in that Rosina wasn't entirely fair to you. Zillah told her in confidence why she ought to go with Keith. He begged her to and the reason was one no wife could dismiss lightly. She wouldn't have kept it from you—Rosina, I mean—except that with you and Melisande being so close, and Melisande knowing mutual friends, she didn't want to take the risk of gossip. It was something that could have put her marriage in jeopardy, and that meant not only *her* happiness, but the children's too. Children need both parents in a secure and unthreatened existence. I know you now well enough to know you'd never mention it to Melisande. This is what happened.'

She told him. Barnabas said, 'I won't hold it against my aunt that she didn't confide in me. It was a ticklish situation, but thanks for telling me now. I won't let on to Rosina that I know.'

Priscilla felt as they put away their papers and walked back through the copse for lunch with Rosina that this marked a new phase in their relationship.

When he was leaving for the shop Barnabas said, 'I'll be all day tomorrow at the shop, so I won't see you. As a matter of fact I won't be out till at least Wednesday of next week. It's Melisande's long weekend off and I'm taking her up to Christchurch to her people, and though we come back Monday night, Tuesday is just bristling with business appointments.'

All the brightness of the day went with him. Priscilla just couldn't return to the study to work. She elected to garden instead, fiercely tackling tasks that took immense physical effort.

Rosina, not without inner amusement, noticed it. At night she said, 'Seeing you won't be working much on the book till Barnabas gets back, how about you having your sister and brother-in-law and family out for the weekend? They could have the chalet and look after themselves. What about it?'

'That would be lovely,' and for once she wasn't thinking of the pleasure it would give the others but the fact that with a crowd about them, she wouldn't be able to miss Barnabas so much. Or think about all they'd talked of this morning, and be tempted to read too much into it. Bother Barnabas and his inner conflicts . . . she wasn't as much as going to think about him this whole weekend. Maybe he was going to try to resolve them, alone with Melisande. And that was a bleak prospect.

Rosina's suggestion had been a happy one. Priscilla felt as if the gates of yesterday had swung back and old happinesses were remembered from the days before Clarice had leaned so heavily on her.

There was a great difference in Clarice. She was fun, as she had been in late childhood, more as she was meant to be before she had been completely spoiled by an over-indulgent mother with an exceptionally pretty child. Roger was good for her, now he had the chance. What was more, Clarice knew it. She said to Priscilla as they lay on the bank of the pool sunbathing, watching Roger swing each child across in turn, on willow branches, 'Priscilla, there's something different about you. I always thought of you as just my sister. You've got more personality now, as if living here looking after these children has satisfied you as nothing else has done. True?'

Priscilla nodded. 'Yes, holding down a secretarial job was just something I did to earn my living. I feel I've only begun to live since coming out here. Clarice, I'm staying on after Zillah Darfield gets back. I'm working on a children's book. I think I've got something. I want to give myself enough time to complete it, and being able to work in the chalet is heaven.'

Clarice's blue eyes went sober. 'You ought to have been able to do this long ago, but I'm afraid I leaned on you too much when Geoff died. I've always felt so inadequate compared with you, Priscilla. You were so capable, so much the mistress of your fate. So sturdy in spirit, even as a small child. I had no confidence in myself, but I have now. Roger's shown me I can do all sorts of things I'd never have as much attempted before. You were always round to do them.

'It's the oddest thing,' she went on. 'Geoff carried on when Mother left off, just pampered me. Then when I married Roger I didn't think it was going to be a success. I knew he loved me, but at times I was miserably conscious that he didn't respect me. I played up a bit, tried for more attention, put on a few sob acts; don't look so surprised at my admitting it, little sister. But suddenly I saw through myself.

'We had a blazing row. Roger said he wanted a helpmeet, not a clinging vine, and that if I wasn't careful I'd spoil the children's lives the way I'd almost spoiled yours. I got an awful shock. Priscilla, tell me, have I done you real harm, or have you got out in time? I mean, there was that awfully nice Miles Standour and but for me I think you'd have made a match of it, but I'm sure he thought you had far too much family responsibility.'

Priscilla's laugh was so spontaneous it was completely convincing. 'Oh, Clarice, you idiot! I gave Miles the push. He was a dear, but too immature to be interesting. He'd have been a leaner too. He just wasn't what I wanted in a man.'

'Well, thank goodness. But I liked that boss of yours. Now there's a man for you. I think he came out to look your family over. I took a great fancy——'

Priscilla held up a hand. 'Hold it, big sister! Just because you've come over all filial mustn't mean you're going to match-make. Barnabas Lockhart was my boss. Now he's my new boss's nephew, that's all. He's practically engaged to the most ravishing blonde, one Melisande Drew. In fact they're spending this weekend with her people in Christ-church, so it's all been imagination on your part, dear. Not to worry, Clarice, there are more things in life than mar-riage and I feel with my feet set on the first rungs of literary success, if Mr Right comes along, I'll just look on him as a bonus.'

Clarice flung an arm round her shoulders, hugged her, said, 'Good for you, little sister. That's what you're going to be from now on. But I'm disappointed about this Barna-bas. But I guess if you'd been interested you'd never have left Lockhart's. Oh, Priscilla, I'm enjoying life as never before. I feel a person in my own right at last, not just a shadow. I'm going to take on some nurse-aiding. I've started some preliminary training . . . Oh, Roger, look out!'

There was a tremendous crack as Roger tried his weight on a branch too light and disappeared in a positive geyser of water. Clarice leapt up, dived, joined him in the pool. Priscilla was glad for Roger and Clarice, glad for the chil-dren. Glad there was now a more natural relationship be-tween herself and her sister. There were always compensa-tions, many of them. Life here in Fair-acre Valley, even if Barnabas married Melisande and lived in town, would give her the new friendships in the village; her work too, even if collaboration with Barnabas wouldn't be without pain, would have its joyous moments. If she had worked with him in the office for twelve months without giving herself away, surely she could continue to do so here, with so much at stake . . . getting established in the world she'd longed to enter. Meanwhile, despite her determination to relegate him to a minor place in her life, it seemed a long time to Wednesday.

Wednesday morning she had a message relayed to her through the dilly Miss Freeman. 'Mr Lockhart's secretary asked me to let you know Mr Lockhart won't be back from Christchurch till next week.'

Priscilla told Rosina in the most casual tone she could summon up as she passed her where she was training some young fuchsias into standard bushes, and went over to the Thistledown House where she worked unceasingly and uninspiredly for two solid hours, then tore up every word she'd written and decided that in the afternoon she'd simply do some typing revision on what she and Barnabas had done together. She couldn't for a moment consider such dull writing as worthy of print.

Dougal and Elspeth were taking Rosina into a flower display in Dunedin, so when she had the house to herself she did something she despised herself for, but couldn't seem to resist . . . she rang the section of the hospital where Melisande worked and said, 'I don't want to speak to her, but I wondered if you could tell me what duty Miss Drew is on this week.'

The answer was what she'd dreaded: 'Oh, Miss Drew is on holiday in Christchurch and isn't expected back till next week.'

So she must make up her mind that their kindred exchanges of conversation, their close co-operative work, their shared likes and dislikes, the two kisses they had shared, meant nothing. She would certainly see to it that they took no more moonlight rambles, did not go as a couple visiting the Manse, or attend evening service together at St Enoch's when, if Barnabas was out here for the week end, Rosina so often pretended twice on Sundays was getting too much for her.

She met Nerolie's mother at an Institute bazaar in Fair-acre. They found themselves at afternoon tea together in the marquee. Mrs Palmerston had bright copper hair (possibly the sign of a quick temper?) and tawny brown eyes and had a delightful voice and manner. Priscilla was cautious, remembering all Nerolie had told Alicia. Inevitably they talked of the children.

Judy Palmerston said, 'Nerolie thinks you're just marvellous—better than some mothers, she said, that you play and swim with them, and don't even mind them helping when you're baking. I think that was one in the eye for me, because the other day I just had to get on—Rob's parents were coming and I was trying to fill the tins so we could have all the time possible with them when they arrived. So I hadn't time.'

Priscilla laughed. 'Of course, with Rosina and me there are two to share the chores. So if I'm baking, I'm not rushing to get done so I can get on with ironing or vacuuming. Mothers sometimes just don't have time.'

'I ought to have it, only it seems to take weeks to settle in a new house, though with only one child, perhaps I'm not organised enough. Nerolie's getting far too introspective. It's good for her to be with Alicia so much. I've always thought it lovely when only children—or any children—have imaginary playmates, but Nerolie overdoes it. She has dozens of them, all the characters of whatever books she's reading. It sometimes drives her father up the wall. It was funny when she was little trying to remember who she was at the moment, like a royal princess or a little girl in the circus, like a trick rider, which gave her an excuse for balancing on the back of a couch and leaping madly through bamboo hoops suspended from trees, but lately she's been imagining herself into the less likable characters, and you find yourself reprimanding her for speaking pertly and get the excuse, in injured tones: "I'm that sarcastic Sabina . . ." So if ever she tries it on with you, do just deflate her. She mustn't trade on it.'

Priscilla laughed, said, 'There's been no sign of that. I expect she's enough sense not to try it on away from home. Isn't it awful the phases children go through?' They gathered up their purchases and departed, Priscilla feeling somewhat relieved. Nerolie's accounts of her home life were probably exercises of the imagination, linked up with some story of misunderstood children.

She had a little talk with Alicia that night, when she was tucking her in. 'Alicia, you know some children have imaginary playmates? Especially only children? They usually only last till they go to school, and it's fun, but sometimes they make these playmates scapegoats for their own naughty doings. Jill used to play this. It was never Jill who left the top off the toothpaste, or tracked mud in, it was always Dina, her imaginary buddy. Till one day when her daddy said that as Dina never got smacked, Jill was going to be so that Dina could see crime didn't pay.'

Alicia giggled. 'And did she stop seeing Dina all the time then?'

'No. We rather liked to hear this little girl talking away to her, so we kept on asking about her, but didn't let her be used as an excuse any more. That's what you call letting your imagination run away with you. Some grown-ups do it even, and call it romancing, but sometimes they can't tell it from truth and that's just sheer lying.

'Now I think your friend Nerolie is a bit that way. She likes having people sorry for her, so she exaggerates what happens to her at home. You're very sympathetic, so if you think she's being punished by not having much lunch, you give her yours. She *could* have nibbled some on the way to school. I really expect that like most parents, they occasionally spank her, but never cruelly, I'm sure.'

Alicia's big blue eyes stared up at Priscilla, then she said slowly and distinctly, 'Nerolie says no one ever believes her about how she gets treated and it's because people don't want to believe those things. I'm very disappointed in you, Priscalla. I thought you were different from most grown-ups.' And she turned her face to the wall. 'Good-night.' Priscilla felt she must leave well alone and just hope some doubt had sunk in.

She went downstairs and told Rosina. Rosina looked worried. 'I can imagine her retreating into her shell. I remember having these passionate loyalties when young, not wanting to see any fault. Don't worry. It will probably be very painful for Alicia if her idol turns out to have feet of clay, but that's one of the things in the school of hard knocks we all have to go through for ourselves. We can't cushion all things for them, unfortunately.'

Priscilla had a sudden longing for Barnabas, with his commonsense outlook. She could hardly march off and ask the Palmerstons was it possible Nerolie's imagination had spread to them? And there were no others in the district who knew these newcomers. She said to Rosina, 'One hint to anyone else and the Palmerstons' reputation would suffer. I must try to get to know Judy better. By now she might be glad to do a bit of visiting. Perhaps we could ask her along some time when Nerolie's here and judge their relationship for ourselves.'

CHAPTER EIGHT

LATE that night the phone rang. Rosina had been in bed some time and Priscilla had sat on, unable to put down a fascinating whodunnit. She answered without enthusiasm. With Barnabas in Christchurch there was such little likelihood of hearing that well-loved voice with its crisp timbre, it didn't matter who rang.

The next moment she was hearing his voice. She was so taken by surprise she couldn't keep the gladness out of her voice. 'Oh, Barnabas, are you back home?'

'No, I'm not, but would you have liked that, Priscilla?'

It caught her unprepared, she hesitated. He laughed. 'Let yourself go, Priscilla. Don't retreat into your shell. Would you have liked that, I said?' There was the most endearingly teasing note in his voice.

She said, 'Yes, I'm dying to get on with the book. I'm just brimming with ideas, but I'm beginning to rely on your sketches being produced on the spot to pep up my own inspiration.'

His chuckle was a disbelieving one. 'I said let yourself go, girl. That's a wishy-washy reason for wishing a chap to return.'

She tried to think of something to head him off. 'How—how is Melisande? Have you had a nice time in Christchurch? Has the weather been kind to you?'

There was a mocking tone in his voice. 'Let me see . . . One, Melisande is very well. She's on top of the world. I've never seen her look more beautiful. Radiant, in fact.'

Priscilla felt as if someone had just dashed cold water over her. He went on, 'Two, we've had a helluva time in Christchurch—crises, too much emotion, family discussions, decisions, decisions, decisions all the way!'

Could he but have seen her, Priscilla was biting her lower lip and clutching the phone till her knuckles were white. What could he mean? Crises? Decisions? Did it mean that their relationship, undetermined till now, had suddenly been resolved? Then why, oh, why had he started off their conversation as he had? Or was he so elated that he hardly knew what he was saying? A man could react like that when the girl who'd once jilted him had finally decided to marry him!

He continued, 'Three, the weather! At its most capricious. It was ironic. The first few days when it didn't matter, it was idyllic, Christchurch at its best, but when it mattered most we settled into two days of fog.'

Priscilla could have shaken him. Even if she'd asked, what did weather really matter? What did were those decisions. Whether he and—Barnabas said, 'Here were we, trying to get Melisande off to London and the airport was closed.'

Priscilla's ears popped and for a moment she could hear nothing but the subsequent drumming in them. Barnabas said, 'Priscilla, are you there? Are we cut off? Can you hear me?'

She swallowed quickly to clear her ears, said, 'I—I—oh, I suppose the line faded a bit.'

'Did you get what I just said?'

She tried to sound ordinary. 'I'm not sure—it was a bit faint. I thought you said something about Melisande going to London. But she wasn't contemplating a trip, was she?'

'No. I was going to leave it to tell you when I came home, but my eye fell on the phone and I found myself picking it up and ringing you. Because I've still got a few days to put in up here. Priscilla, Melisande has been through a very tough time the last three years. You'd never have guessed. This is confidential. I'll just tell you and Rosina.

'She fell deeply in love with a surgeon, but there was no future to it. She and I had kept company some time previously—one of those sort of attachments drifted into, no spark in it, just partnering each other to things, and we'd broken it off. Melisande had fallen for someone else, but it didn't last. Then she met Donald. His wife had been incurably crippled for years. Melisande may sound a flibbertygibbet, but she's got a high standard of morality. Even her pity for him and her longing to help him didn't sweep her off her feet.

'She worked so closely with him she was afraid it would become apparent, so we agreed I should squire her round, so no one should guess. I certainly admired those two. They deserve a medal. Finally, Donald felt it was completely unfair to her, that she was wasting her life. He took a position in England that gave a chance, a faint chance, of improvement for his wife in a clinic nearby. It gave her ease for a year, but no cure.

'She died a few months ago. They set themselves a date for the end of the year, to meet again here in New Zealand. But when we were in Christchurch, he rang Melisande. He was so desperately lonely he said she must come to him immediately. Her father and mother were delighted. They'd spoiled her somewhat as a child, and this—the fact that she loved someone not free to marry her—the one thing they couldn't give her . . . happiness, had nearly killed them.

'I thought it was a pity they couldn't be at her wedding, so I managed to persuade them to go with her. Her father's in the same line as me, but in the wholesale trade, so I was able to help him with some commitments. That's what kept me. I booked their flights, fortunately they had passports, and they were all set to go when this fog delayed things. Anyway, they got away for Auckland today, though even then they were delayed. However, I had a ring from Melisande ten minutes ago to say they were taking off almost immediately. They'll be heading Honolulu-wise any moment and all my worries are over. It really meant something to see those three people depart from Harewood Airport, looking completely happy.'

Priscilla felt as if happiness was breaking over her in a wave too, but she mustn't read too much into the fact that he had immediately rung her. But ... well, at least they were kindred, shared the same interests, loved the same things, were about to produce a book together ... perhaps at last she might dare hope.

Barnabas said, 'I'm still at their house on Cashmere Hills. They don't want to leave it unoccupied, so they're having tenants who won't arrive till Sunday. I'm to see them in, get a bond from them, get the contract signed. I'll be home in three days. That's one complication out of the way. How about you?'

She didn't know how to take him.

Her voice was breathless. 'How about me? In what way? I didn't know my life was in any way complicated. At least not any more, not since coming to Jesmond Dene. I've been feeling very ... oh, how shall I put it? ... uncluttered.'

She meant she no longer had a clinging vine of a sister to consider. That Clarice and the children were now completely Roger's responsibility.

'Uncluttered?' he repeated. 'Yes, as good a way of putting it as any. You mean no remnants of past ties cling now?'

'That's what I mean.' Oh, how she wished this wasn't being conducted at a distance of over two hundred miles! She wished she was face to face with him so she could read his expression.

He laughed. 'That's enough to go on with. Priscilla, I wrote you about this last night, when I finally got to bed, but I've not posted the letter. I got carried away and said too much. I'd rather tell you the things that were in it—there's much less room for misunderstanding than in the written word. Listen, the worst of it is that I'll not be able to see you as soon as I get back. That'll be Monday. I'll leave Christchurch early but will have to go straight to the shop. I wasn't prepared to be away so long and I've had to be constantly on toll-calls with business details. They're holding back the ads for the morning paper, so I'll have to okay them, then get it across to the *Times*, then work flat out on other backlog stuff to be prepared to receive travellers all day Tuesday. But I'll see you that evening, when all the fret and fuss of the day is over. But leave Tuesday night completely free, won't you?'

'Oh, I will. It'll be easy. I'm spending as much time as possible on *Ambrosina* now. Barnabas, I must go. This must be costing you a fortune.'

'Who cares, even if it's only a next-best thing? It's a glorious night here. Out of the window in this hill suburb I can see all Christchurch spread before me on the Canterbury plains. There's such a moon you can even see a glint of silver in a long line that's the hint of snow on the Southern Alps. It's magnificent. You ought to be here.'

'The little Taieri Plain will do me . . . so much smaller, so much more intimate, really, with the Maungatuas almost rising out of Rosina's garden. Barnabas, goodnight, sleep well.'

'I will now I've heard your voice. Goodnight, Priscilla.' She sat on, bemused, going over every word, allowing herself to dream of all it might mean, then caught herself up for reading what she wanted to read into it. Then she laughed a little low laugh, because *of course* there was meaning in it and warmth and promise of a happy ending. She felt her fingers were almost curving round his fingers, even though all those miles separated them.

Why shouldn't she dream? She'd agonised plenty over the situation when he seemed far beyond her reach. The window was still open and the perfumes of Rosina's garden swept in, balsam, mint, lavender, mignonette, roses . . . she and Barnabas would have those fragrances drifting in night after night, through their bedroom window. Rosina would realise a dream too and go to live at Thistledown House, just through the larches. Near but not too near; Rosina was so wise.

Their children, hers and Barnabas's, would play on those front steps, pat the mossy figures on them, slide down these banisters inside, climb the Wellingtonia, the Iron Duke as Rosina called it, get hooked on it, too. Oh, just imagine,

had she not offered to deliver that mail for her boss, none
of this might have happened.

Priscilla went out into the night, strolled between the
fuchsias, the Chinese Crackers, the Victor Hugos, the dainty
Crinolines, the robust Commanders-in-chief, the delicate
beauty of the Grey Ladies, the Leonoras, the Sweet Annies.
All named and precious. What a great-aunt Rosina would
make, their Lady of the Fuchsias, flitting round them
lovingly in purple dusks and golden sunrises. She walked
on scattered rose-petals on the flagged paths. Barnabas
had quoted the last rose of summer to her . . . but still they
bloomed. Come winter, who knows what might have happened? Possibly there'd be no more long, lonely nights.
Winter would be a delightful time, shut snugly into the
sturdy walls of Jesmond Dene. How glad her grandfather
would have been for her, living in a house whose name was
a link with his loved Tyneside. They would have aromatic
logs burning as Manuel had, there would be chairs drawn
close to the blaze, a world for two. Priscilla laughed to herself, decided she *must* go to bed. She mustn't be so reluctant
to ring the curtain down on this enchanted evening because
there would be others, more enchanted still, and fair tomorrows.

Priscilla knew she must give nothing away to Rosina next
morning. She gave her no hint that Barnabas had con-
veyed anything but the news of Melisande's approaching
wedding to her and the probable time of his return.

Rosina was unashamedly relieved. 'He's always been far
too chivalrous towards Melisande. Mind you, I respect her
more now, but she was still using him, and she wouldn't
care that it must have seemed to everyone as if they were
going to make a match of it after all.'

Priscilla said slowly, 'It did seem tough on him, but
Melisande is a proud girl, and we do strange things to save
our pride. If they'd known each other from childhood, he'd
be used to picking her up and bandaging, so he'd just con-

tinue on.' There was something she just had to ask. 'When,
as you once told me, she jilted him, was he broken up?'

Rosina laughed. 'No, that's why I didn't want to see
them drifting together again. I know she's a beauty, the
sort men turn and stare after, but Barnabas was never on
cloud nine about her. It wasn't just that they'd known each
other all their lives, because Manuel and I knew each other
from the time I was seven, but there was always magic
there. It's an odd thing, that. The vital spark. That's why
you see such seemingly oddly assorted couples making a
real go of marriage. Something in one calls to the other.
It's quite undefinable. It was never there with Melisande
and Barnabas.'

Priscilla found it hard not to burst into song as she went
about their daily tasks. She swept, dusted, made the meals,
gardened madly. It had to be the sheer joy of physical
work today. She couldn't settle at her desk.

How long the days were going to seem till he came
home! How maddening that so much work awaited him. If
only he could have called in . . . but he seemed to want to
have the demanding urgency of his backlog of appointments
behind him, to come to her in the leisure and peace of this
old-world garden.

Rosina looked at her. 'Priscilla, how much longer are you
going to stand there with the shears in your hand? You
look like Lot's wife!'

Priscilla started, came back to reality, said, 'All writers
get like this, Rosina, lost in plotting.'

Rosina said rather suavely, 'Yes, of course. What else
could it be? You plot on, if it makes you look so happy, but
you won't cut that pink *manuka* clean down, will you? I
only wanted the straggly stuff clipped off it.' She hid a
smile.

It was impossible not to plan their meeting. She hoped
he'd ring, so they might be alone, with not even Rosina.
Nice if he asked her to wait for him at Thistledown, where
not even a phone call could break in; or down at the willow-

shaded pool with the late sunlight shining on the haystack beyond, and the lovely curve of a green mountain reaching down to meet the clover and daisies of the meadow. But so often the big moments of life were not idyllic. They got sandwiched in between household disasters which were a-plenty in the world of Nat, Tim, and Alicia.

If he got through quickly and came out for dinner, he'd probably arrive when Tim fell in the liquid manure again, or when they were all engaged in fisticuffs or verbal warfare.

That evening Priscilla was really restless. She'd finished her library book, there was nothing worth watching on television, and it was no use suggesting Scrabble because Rosina was poring over a rose catalogue. How absurd to want a library book with these shelves bulging with treasures! She went across to them, and presently drew out a fat black scrapbook. 'Rosina, is this private? Or may I dip into it? It seems full of clippings of poetry, and I'm just in the mood for that. It looks so intriguing. Things were stuck in here when events that are now history were happening in the world. There's a speech here given in 1935 by Mussolini, making the ridiculous statement that war is to men what childbirth is to women. When one gives life, the other destroys it! And there are bits about Edward the Eighth's Abdication, the first ones stuck in when it wasn't even resolved. But I can see things in your handwriting, so it could be private.'

'Dear child, there may be the odd personal bit, but I've never been one for keeping a day-to-day diary—only jotted down a few moods and impressions at times when I felt the need of expressing myself in the written word, and in any case, you would understand. You might even get a few *Ambrosina* ideas. The Abdication! I can't even think of it now without a stab of the heart. But deeply as I felt it, it hurt my father more. It was a personal grief to him, like the grief and devotion of some to Bonnie Prince Charlie. I'll never forget my father saying to me, "Rose, he *won't* do this to us, will he?" Aye, he was gallant to the last, our uncrowned King, and sorely beset. There's a lot of history and pain and joy bound up in these pages. But two glorious reigns have followed.

'On the less serious side you'll find some nonsense verses. My father used to say to garner all we could of laughter and joy, especially in little things, then when the big things in life failed us, we'd find compensations because we were in the habit of enjoying small blessings. I never get over missing my father. Even at this age, I find myself wanting to tell him things. Oh, Priscilla, I'm making you cry.'

'Don't worry, Rosina. I liked that because it's just the way I feel with Dad. At times I ache to hear his voice. Yet he wouldn't like me to over-grieve.'

'But if a man like Seth wasn't missed, there'd be something wrong with his family. In a very real way men of his calibre and my father's calibre are still with us in their influence on our lives. I often feel as if yesterday reaches on ahead of us into tomorrow. Because occasionally, some vivid thought of Manuel seems as if it was just waiting for me. I have to decide something and suddenly I feel he's just round the corner out of sight among the trees, and I know exactly what he'd think was best for me.'

Priscilla said softly, 'It must be the best life has to offer, having known that sort of bond.'

Rosina chuckled for some reason. 'I know it is, but the last thing I'd want to create, Priscilla, is the image of perfection between Manuel and myself. That's unfair to young people starting out on life together. Because it's only as you go it becomes more idyllic. Manuel and I often had flare-ups. I was such a passionate creature, with strong loyalties and wild crazes. Manuel was more slowly geared and often I'd be impatient with him because he wasn't championing my causes with the same impetuous enthusiasms. Sometimes I found his slower way best, but I took so long to learn.'

Priscilla had brought the scrapbook to the table. Rosina's

crêpey hand was lying on it. Priscilla leaned over and patted it. 'But sometimes your more eager way would be best. Not all impulses should be curbed. Sometimes it would be a crime not to fly instantly to someone's defence. So you each complemented the other.'

Rosina said, 'I can't think how I existed before you came to Jesmond Dene, child.'

'I felt old beyond my years before I did. You make me feel younger, more irresponsible, Ambrosina Claremont. I've never been so happy in my life.'

They became absorbed in their reading again. Priscilla turned a page, read:

'PLANNING

I had planned the meeting of us,
    Glad beneath a starlit sky,
Swift compelling arms around me,
    While enchanted moments fly.

I had thought of things to tell you,
    Only you could understand,
As we walked our way together
    In a rare enchanted land.

But you came an hour too early,
    And the kitchen floor was wet,
I was elbow deep in dishes
    And my hair was in a net.

As I wrung the soapy dishcloth
    My romance was all a wreck,
And for one hot bothered second
    I'd have rather wrung your neck.
                                    —Sonia Hardie'

Priscilla's laughter rang out like a golden bell. What would it matter *when* Barnabas came? One had to see the funny side. But she hoped their meeting wouldn't be an anti-climax like that. She wouldn't satisfy Rosina's curiosity, shaking her head. 'Darling, there are some things it's not good for you to know . . . yet.'

She expected her to persist, but Rosina contented herself with saying, 'I've lived too long to be impatient now. Manuel taught me that if you bide your time, things grow richer.' Priscilla's lone dimple cleaved her left cheek. 'Could be I'll tell you next week.'

The phone rang—Clarice. Priscilla was surprised at the pleasure she had these days in hearing her sister's voice.

'Priscilla, Roger and I have this weekend free and alone. The children are going up to stay with their friends at Middlemarch. If it's convenient to you, and only if it is, we'd like to come out for the weekend. We'd bring our own linen and supplies—we don't want to make more work for you. Roger's off south next week, and I can't go because I've got visitors coming, but a weekend at the Thistledown House would be gorgeous.'

'I'd love it, Clarice. I'll just ask Rosina.' She came back. 'Rosina would love it too. But don't bring linen—with an automatic washing-machine it's the work of a moment to pop sheets and towels in, and you can eat over here with us, bar breakfast. Give us the pleasure of preparing for you. See you tomorrow night, then.'

It was something to do, to fill in the time till Barnabas should come to set the wheels of the universe turning again for Priscilla. When the weekend was over there would be only Monday to get through. Oh, joy, joy!

Priscilla said to Rosina next day, 'I think that at last the friendship between Nerolie and Alicia is getting on to a better footing. Nerolie is writing stories. She and Alicia have been reading your *Anne of Green Gables* books and are forming a Story Club like Anne and her friends did. I feel if the yarns Nerolie spreads are just inventions, then this will give her imagination an outlet. I was getting in the washing today and they were up in the crotch of the peartree, eating and talking. They had no idea I was there at first. They were spinning each other the stories they were going to write in their new exercise books. Alicia's story was true to type, she was saving friends from untold disasters. Nerolie's was weirdly and wonderfully involved— a stolen child, brought up not knowing she was heiress to a fortune and a castle, dozens of improbable coincidences and a lot of skulduggery, with all the villains impossibly black-hearted and the goodies lily-white. Finally the child escapes and hides in a hut in the grounds of the castle and recognises her mother.

'They came down, discussed it with me, because I'm a writer. I took them seriously and managed to suggest it's a good idea to write a story with a setting they know, that it's easier to describe someone lost in New Zealand bush than in the middle of the New Forest. I had to laugh. "Experience, that's what we need," said Nerolie, "but it takes so long to get it." I laughed and said experience would come to them soon enough, but how about imagining little pioneer girls, coming to New Zealand on a sailing-ship in 1848 and landing at Dunedin and their fathers taking up land on the Taieri when it was covered in flax and swamp and the hills thick with bush. It would be so easy for one of them to get lost in it. They've just had this at school and it would be a good exercise for them.'

'So it will. I'll look forward to seeing their efforts. It could easily direct Nerolie's vivid imagination—because I'm sure that's what it is, from exaggerating the discipline of her home. Then Alicia won't get her feelings lacerated.'

They had a snack and retired to bed, Priscilla to lie awake for a blissful hour dreaming in her attic among the purple and silver stripes, the little gilt cherubs and blue ribbon knots of the days to come.

They had a happy weekend. Priscilla felt she hadn't seen her sister so relaxed and contented for years. It hardly seemed possible that after years of grizzling and working on other people's sympathies to get them to perform duties for her, Clarice was now patently enjoying being thought capable. She carried herself more erectly, didn't flop all over the place and even her voice held eagerness instead of a whine.

Alicia's cup was overflowing because Priscilla had rung Mrs Palmerston and Nerolie was allowed to stay for Saturday night. The two girls retired to an old barn where they had set up a table for a desk, and orange-boxes to hold their paper and ballpoints, and were writing their stories with great gusto.

Just before Roger and Clarice retired to Thistledown on Saturday night, and they were having a last cup of tea, Roger said, 'That child Nerolie reminds me of someone, I can't think who. Are they local people?'

'Yes, but newcomers. Her surname is Palmerston. Her father is the new postmaster here—oh, might you have met him in your work?' Roger was a Post Office supervisor in the engineers' department.

He snapped his fingers. 'That's it! I knew him in Christchurch years ago. She's dark like him. The mother—a lovely girl—was a redhead. What a brick she was! She lost two babies before she had this one, and was so determined to have a child she spent almost five months in hospital beforehand.'

Rosina and Priscilla looked at each other, burst out laughing. 'Then Nerolie's imagination does get away with her,' said Priscilla. 'She plays on Alicia's sympathy with weird tales of ill-treatment. She said it was because her mother never wanted her. I think I'm going to have a word with Miss Nerolie and let her know it's not fair to her parents to dramatise herself like this, that it's got to stop. I hope her parents never know. But I don't think she's said anything except to Alicia. She told her not to tell anyone because she was so ashamed!'

She made an opportunity the next day. She hated having to do it in front of Alicia, but that had to be done. She brought animal biscuits and lemonade into the barn, said, laughing, 'I'm bringing this in, not the maid, because she might interrupt your train of thought, but as your secretary, I felt I wouldn't intrude so much.'

Nerolie's eyes sparkled. 'Oh, do you like to pretend too?'

'Of course she does,' said Alicia. 'She's a writer too. She told me the other day she—um—identifies herself so much with her characters that if they're in the middle of a snow-storm, even if it's summer, she shivers too, and if they're hungry, she gets hungry.'

'I'm like that,' said Nerolie with relish. 'I get absolutely terrified if the girl I'm writing about is lost in the middle of a spooky wood, with ghostly fingers clutching at her as she rushes through it, her long hair streaming in the wind, and it sends shudders up and down my spine and brings me out in goose-pimples. Priscilla, why is being scared to death with stories you're reading or making up sort of—um———'

'Sort of enjoyable?' she twinkled.

'Yes, isn't it funny?'

Priscilla nodded. 'But it's best not to get too worked up about it. I overdid it once. My mum and dad were worried about me. I began to do everything with my left hand and I wasn't left-handed. When they asked me I was too em-barrassed to say I was imagining myself a little girl with only one arm. They thought my right arm must be sore and took me to our doctor. He was a very wise old doctor and instead of taking tests, he sent my parents out of the room and just said quietly, "You've got a reason for it, haven't you, Priscilla, only you're afraid everyone will laugh at you, but it doesn't matter, you can tell me." So I told him. He didn't tell my parents in front of me, just said it didn't matter, but thought it was a good thing to use both hands equally and it was called ambi-dexterous, but I mustn't let other people worry because of my imagination. He rang Dad on the quiet and told him and nobody laughed and hurt my feelings by saying what a duffer I was.'

Priscilla looked at Nerolie and said, 'Just as no one's going to call you a duffer for spreading such stories about your mother and father. But *we've* got to stop looking as if we believed them. *You've* had your fun out of imagining them. Your mother wanted a baby so much she spent almost five months in hospital before you were born so you'd be full time and not be delicate. They needn't know, as long as it was only Alicia you romanced to. But we've got to draw the line between romancing and truth. Especially if it would hurt other people.'

Nerolie gazed at her, the picture of guilt. Out of the corner of her eye Priscilla had seen Alicia's fair skin flush scarlet, then pale again. Poor Alicia, disillusionment was hard to bear at nine. Being made a fool of was worst of all. Priscilla held her breath, prayed she'd done the right thing. Children could really suffer over these things.

Of a sudden Alicia flung her head back, glared at Nerolie, said, 'You absolute nit! I ought to bash you one. But I can't be bothered. I think you're dippy. I'd rather imagine nice things than horrid things any day. I just hope you aren't going to write stories like that. Mine are all going to have happy endings!'

'Well, so are mine,' said Priscilla, hoping to divert attention away from Nerolie's perfidy, 'but they have to have lots of adventures first. This little pioneer girl who gets lost fights her way into a pocket of bush in the Maungatuas, say, and just when she's desperate, she could stumble on a little clearing and find a chalet like this built by a Swiss goldminer.'

Alicia objected. 'They didn't find gold in Otago in the very first days. Not till 1861.'

Nerolie looked impressed. 'Well, have you got any other ideas why he'd be there?' She must win her way into Alicia's favour again. Alicia looked stumped.

'He could be a whaler,' suggested Priscilla. 'The whaling ships were round this coast long before any pioneers arrived. But I suppose he couldn't be Swiss—theirs is a land-locked country, isn't it? Perhaps he could be a German. I think they have these kind of houses in their mountains.

He could be eccentric but lovable, so not too scary.'

Nerolie took it up, 'She could be here two whole days and nights on her own, because he was away exploring. It would be black dark at nights and there'd only be candles for light and owls would hoot and she'd be very brave.'

'She'd be scared out of her wits,' said Alicia. 'I would be.'

'Pooh ... she would not. She'd be like me. I wouldn't turn a hair,' said Nerolie. Priscilla left them arguing enjoyably and thought with an inward grin that Barnabas had been right about Nerolie all along.

Roger and Clarice were entranced with Barnabas's illustrations and were sure the joint venture was going to be a great success. Priscilla, to her surprise, found herself even showing Clarice her text.

Rosina said, 'This is very good for Barnabas. He must have found it frustrating at times to not be able to express himself with brush and colour.'

Priscilla said, 'Not that it's easy now. He's had to concertina his work at the shop to get it in.'

'Oh, you can nearly always find time for what you want most to do,' said Roger, 'in fact not so much find time as make it.'

Rosina said slyly, 'And now, of course, the incentive is much greater. He'll make the time all right. He can hardly bear to stay away.'

Roger and Clarice looked at her, then at Priscilla who felt the colour come up in her cheeks. She bent over the sketches. 'Yes, knowing I've had some stuff already published makes him keen—he feels we can collaborate with some hope of success.'

Roger looked wicked. 'Well, it's as good a name as any other for it, collaborating, and very enjoyable too, in this set-up.'

Priscilla changed the subject. 'By the way, Roger, you needn't run Clarice in tomorrow morning. Rosina has decided to take some nerine bulbs in to a friend in Roslyn and will take her with her. They have to be moved when they're in flower, you know. As you're going to Invercargill, it will save you quite a bit of time.'

'Oh, good. I hate retracing tracks, even for you, Clarice. I can cut straight south from here past the airport. I suppose you know it means a fairly early start, Rosina? Clarice has a man coming to cut the hedge at nine, Oh, thanks a lot. Sure it's not too early for you? Good, it couldn't be better.'

Priscilla thought so too, because she had so much to do. Had she only known, that small decision couldn't have been a worse one.

Clarice and Rosina got away before Roger did. When they'd waved them off, she went over to the Thistledown House with Roger. She'd promised to do their breakfast dishes, strip the bed, take the linen back to the big house to wash it.

She took a hasty look round the bedroom. 'You haven't forgotten anything? Packed your pyjamas, got your razor in? Oh, what about your book?'

'I finished it last night. Rosina wants the loan of it. You might give it to her.'

'Very well, that appears to be all, so you're away, Roger, you needn't take the car past the house. The other track leads through to the main road and brings you nearer the village and instead of going through it, take the first road to the left, and it joins the airport road a mile or two on. I don't think I'll stay over here yet. I've things to do at the other house.'

They went down the stairs, Priscilla carrying his holdall, Roger his case.

CHAPTER NINE

BARNABAS LOCKHART had, after all, managed to leave Christ-church on Sunday, but late, so that it was eleven before he reached Tyne Hill. His longing to see Priscilla had kept him from sleeping well, and he'd risen early, determined to see her before the shop claimed him for the day.

He timed it so he could reach Jesmond Dene after the children had left for school and Rosina and Priscilla would be on their own. Rosina would tactfully disappear, he knew. One indication of his head, and she'd make an excuse.

He wasted no time in reaching Fair-acre Valley. He stopped his car in front of the steps, saw the garage door open and Rosina's car gone. Thank heaven Priscilla's car was there. Better and better. The gods were smiling upon him.

The door was open. He bounded up the steps calling her name as he went. She wasn't there. He tore upstairs, came down again. She couldn't be far, probably over at the chalet—nicer still. He made his way through the larch-wood, came to the verge of it. There was the chalet and an opulent-looking car was parked outside it. The door was open.

He could hear voices, very faintly. What made him halt inside the screen of trees he didn't know. He saw Priscilla come out with Roger, tall, brown, happy-looking.

Roger opened a car door, threw in his case, took the holdall from Priscilla, smiled down on her to say something. She sparkled at him, laughed, nodded. He laughed back, bent down, took her face between his hands and kissed her. Not lingeringly but on the lips.

He strode round to the far door, opened it, then called out over the roof of the car so that his voice came quite clearly to Barnabas Lockhart, 'Well, thanks for a most memorable weekend. Take care of yourself.'

Barnabas's jaw was set, his hands clenched. Just as he was about to step out from the trees and confront them, Priscilla called, 'Oh, just a moment, Roger, I'll ride down to the gate with you, save you opening and shutting it. Then I'll walk round to the Dene gate and get our mail. It comes early.' She whipped open the door and got in.

As soon as they were round the bend, Barnabas walked swiftly across to the picket gate, into the chalet and up the spiral stair to the landing outside the master bedroom. He stood in the doorway and looked, his face expressionless.

An unmade double bed with pale blue sheets. Two pillows with imprints of heads that had lain there. A book by the bedside table. He picked it up almost automatically, opened it. On the fly-leaf was scrawled *Roger Whitfield*. He put it down, walked out. He got a glimpse of the breakfast bar that divided kitchen from lounge. Breakfast for two, or the remains. Two plates, two cereal dishes, two cups and saucers.

He walked out into the morning gilded with sunlight, sweet with birdsong and the purling brook, fragrant with the essences of dew and bloom, and didn't see or hear or smell any of it. He was blind and deaf to beauty, blind with anger. He dare not meet her yet. He'd be able to get away before she even reached the bend in the lane that hid the gateway of Thistledown House from that of Jesmond Dene. He wouldn't go through the village, he'd take that side road through Outram. . . .

Priscilla came happily along the lane, smiled reminiscently at the seat round the chestnut, turned in the wrought iron gates, nodded back happily to the fuchsias that seemed to nod to her, and gave a little skip of pure happiness. Had there ever been a lovelier summer? Now autumn was upon them and would be lovelier still. She would go in and make the children's beds, then back to Thistledown House to make it all ready against Barnabas's coming. How lovingly she would dust, how she would enjoy filling the vases ... because tomorrow night he would come to her and she need have no feelings of guilt about Melisande. She would take what life had to offer her with both hands, here in this most delectable spot of all ... Fair-acre Valley.

Tuesday was a fair and lovely day. Priscilla had thought it would never come, but here it was, dew-fresh, with a hint of heat to come in the cloudless sky over the Maungatuas. Priscilla sang to herself as she tripped along to the village, basket on arm.

Had Fair-acre Valley ever looked lovelier? There was still a blacksmith's shop, a green-and-white pub with a village green beside it, an immense chestnut tree with a horse tethered beneath it. Elspeth MacNab's Village Improvement Society had planted the triangle at the crossroads with petunias in pink and purple and white and scarlet so they made a living patchwork, and the row of shops on the bank that rose up from the road had their modern parking area divided from it by beds of phlox drummondii bordered with purple alyssum.

St Enoch's church reared its miniature steeple against a hill clad with English trees that were a glory in autumn, and around the old kirkyard were poplars and beeches. Two huge Wellingtonias as symmetrical as the steeple kept twin guard over the peaceful dwellings of the dead. So many of the names there corresponded with the names of the people in the village and on the farms. Fourth and fifth generation of the pioneers now ... it gave you a sense of continuity.

What a wonderful setting in which to rear children ... oh dear, her thoughts were taking the same trend again ... she called at the butcher's for steak in case Barnabas got away from the shop in time for dinner. He could ring, and she must be ready in case. Reuben Swallow, an immense man, girded in a blue-and-white striped apron, cut the slices with a pleasure in his work that made him an artist at it.

'Beautiful beef ... mature, not aged ... don't overcook it now. Brown it well on the outside and have it palest pink in the centre so it retains its juices. Potatoes in their jackets, I'd say, not French fries. I take it you're having visitors if you're getting this much? Now, I can give you something special to go with it. Just a moment.' He disappeared through a doorway and she could hear him calling, 'Mother? Mother?' with a gusto that would have done credit to Gabriel summoning up the dead.

Little Mrs Swallow appeared behind him. 'Yes, Reuben? Oh, it's Priscilla. How are you, my dear, and Rosina and the children? Tell them I've found that musical box I promised them when you dropped in with them the other day. My, when their mother comes back she'll see how well they've been looked after.'

Reuben said, 'Priscilla and Rosina are having company for dinner tonight. She's taking steak and I thought what would be nicer with it than those button mushrooms you picked on the hill this morning.'

Priscilla's protests were overruled. Mrs Swallow's bright eyes glinted. 'Now, would the company include her nephew? Then you must have the mushrooms. He's a favourite with us. I try not to see him in his shop when I go into town, because he always insists on giving me discount.'

'I'm not sure if he'll be here for the evening meal or not. He's been away in Christchurch on business and rang us to say he hopes to get out to see us in the evening. He's got a very full day in the shop, and may even work on a bit, but I thought I'd be prepared in case. He was just getting back late last night.'

Reuben said. 'Well now, I must have been mistaken. I was taking the shutters down yesterday morn when I thought I saw him driving past—towards Jesmond Dene. Whoever it was honked and waved. I must have been mistaken. I did think it early for him to be out here.'

The mushrooms were beautiful, still dew-fresh. Priscilla went on to the baker's, bought new crisp rolls, and at the store got a bunch of celery because theirs wasn't ready yet, a square of honeycomb. Not that she'd use that today, but Barnabas loved it. It would do for another time. She picked up a packet of China bud tea; he liked his tea strong, but with a pinch of China buds to give it an aroma.

As she walked past the Manse Dougal opened his study window, called out, 'Come on in and have some coffee, Elspeth's just called me for it.'

In she went, Dougal saying as they entered the kitchen, 'Look what's just blown in ... looking as emerald as a shamrock leaf in that vivid green.'

Elspeth was always glad to see Priscilla. She had a smudge of flour on her nose, a batch of scones steaming under a snowy tea-towel, big pottery mugs on the table. She got another mug, buttered the scones, spread strawberry jam on them. 'What a crop we had this year! Danny's proving a scientific gardener and it's giving results. The uncles were out fishing yesterday at Taieri Mouth and came back with flounders. They've got them already for deep freezing. They've filleted them. Could you do with some?'

'Oh, I could do an entrée with those, if Barnabas does make it for dinner tonight. He's just got back from Christchurch. But he's so busy at the shop today, it could be twilight before he gets here.'

She surprised a knowing look on Elspeth's face, added hastily, 'He's such an attentive nephew. I think that with her children all being overseas, he has her on his mind.'

She saw the corners of Dougal's mouth twitch. 'He certainly must have. I've never known him out here so much.'

Priscilla looked down. 'Well, I expect that since she's had the responsibility of the Darfield children too, he's felt he must keep an even closer eye on her.'

'Aye, that would be the way of it,' said the Reverend Dougal MacNab. Then he said, 'You know Melisande Drew is off to London to be married?'

Priscilla was surprised. 'Oh, did Barnabas ring you from Christchurch too?'

'No, from Tyne Hill to tell me. I knew the Drews very well when they lived in Dunedin. It's a good thing she's settled at last. Barney's been very good to her, too good really. He helped Melisande over a bad patch. But it gives folk false ideas to see a man always out with the same girl.' He looked straight at Priscilla. 'For instance, when you were his secretary, I'll guarantee you thought they'd make a match of it. Did you?'

Priscilla felt she must be honest. 'I did. It seemed to me all the staff did.'

Again his look was direct. 'But you know now there was nothing in it. I'd like to think Barney made that clear to you. Did he?'

Priscilla knew she was going pink, but it didn't matter with these dear, dear people. She said, 'He did—very plain, Dougal. On the phone from Christchurch the night she flew away.'

Elspeth, green eyes shining, said, 'Oh, Dougal MacNab, it's pleased I am with you, right now. I've been wanting Priscilla to know that it meant nothing for some time now, but I was afraid I might put my foot in it, be a little premature. So thank you, darling.'

Dougal said, 'We'll leave it at that. It was just that Barnabas Lockhart is my best friend and I wouldn't like him to get his affairs into the sort of snarl Elspeth and I did for the lack of a little frankness. If only some mutual friend had told me of the situation she'd got dragged into through sheer goodness of heart, I'd never have thought what I did. It's a wonder she did marry me when she knew what I'd been thinking.'

Elspeth said, 'Dope! I thought it superb that you still wanted to marry me, thinking that. We'll tell you the whole story some time, Priscilla, when you and Barnabas are here together. Right now I'm more interested in you and——'

Priscilla held up a hand. 'There's nothing to tell yet.'

Elspeth brightened at the final word. 'But there is some-

thing? Oh, please say there is. Dougal, don't look so forbidding. I do want to know.'

Priscilla said slowly, 'Just that he seemed to want me to
know he'd just been helping Melisande out. And that—oh,
how shall I put it? He asked me, more or less, if there was
anyone in my life? If I was free, I suppose he meant—though
it was odd.'

'It's not odd to me,' said Elspeth decidedly. 'Oh, I'm so
thrilled I could turn a somersault!'

Dougal looked alarmed. 'Not here, my love—there's just
not room. And don't let that inspire you to turn one on the
back lawn. This parish is very indulgent towards their unorthodox minister's wife, but there are limits.'

Priscilla was laughing, then she looked rueful. 'It's all so
airy-fairy. I ought not to have said a thing. So——'

Dougal said, 'We'll keep it entirely to ourselves. The last
thing you'd want is for anyone to assume too much just
now. I was well aware of Barnabas's feelings the night you
were with him—I know him so well. But *you* didn't give
anything away. *We* precipitated this discussion, but only
because we didn't want you to have any doubts about Melisande. Well, I must go back to my study and the minor
prophets. I don't think Barney's the kind to let the grass
grow under his feet once it's got to this stage, Priscilla.' He
flicked her cheek with a finger and left them.

Elspeth brought out the package of fillets, slid it into
Priscilla's basket and walked to the gate with her. Somehow they were loth to part. 'It's so lovely having you here,'
Elspeth said. 'Not just because you're a writer too, but that
adds to it. I feel sure your joint venture will be a great
success. How odd. I don't think Barnabas had any idea you
were a writer, or you that he was an artist, when you were
at Lockharts, did he? Did you?'

'No, it was a complete surprise to me when he sketched
in the small *Ambrosina*. It opened up a new world. The sort
of writing I do really does need an illustrator on the spot.
Two months ago I wasn't a very happy person at all. I knew

I must get away from the shop, but after so many years of bearing big responsibilities that needed a good salary, I was scared.'

'Priscilla, why *must* get away? Your burdens had lessened when Clarice married Roger. You could have just moved to a flat at the other end of town, and carried on doing your writing in your spare time. So why did you want to leave?'

Priscilla decided on frankness. It couldn't matter now. 'It was quite corny . . . the old situation of the secretary falling for her boss. It appeared as if he was on the point of getting engaged to someone else, a raving beauty at that. I didn't know how to carry on, tamping down feelings that were threatening to swamp me, betray me. You see, Elspeth, it was the first time I'd ever been in love. I'd been out with quite a few men from time to time, but none ever touched my heart.' She laughed. 'I'd begun to think I was a cold sort of fish, but not any more. I've learned a lot about myself this year.'

Elspeth looked most surprised. 'Cold? You? Oh, Priscilla, you're so vital, so warm. The way you understand those Darfield imps, and love them to death, and manage Rosina . . . but I know how you felt just the same about it being unbearable to be so closely connected and to have to hide your feelings. I was living next to the Manse and Dougal's housekeeper left. I couldn't do anything but look after the household, and I was burning up with love of Dougal, and thought I wouldn't dare marry him. Anyway, leaving us aside, you upped and offed, then, all unknowing, landed on his aunt's doorstep. It's gorgeous! What a marvellous start to a romance!'

'If that's what it is. I'm almost afraid . . .'

'Of course you are. Even in these days, women are still afraid of hoping till a man declares himself. But if he asked was there anyone else in your life that's enough for me. Oh, here's Father O'More coming to see Dougal. Well, he'll rescue him from stewing over the minor prophets. As a rule Dougal gets a thrill out of study, but it's not a favourite subject by any means, only Fergus MacKinnon wanted him to do a series on them and Dougal loves Fergie. Goodbye for now, Priscilla, and stay confident till you see Barnabas.'

Priscilla felt as if she walked home on winged feet.

They were halfway through their lunch before Priscilla noticed that Rosina was very quiet. But she'd not had much chance to be anything else. Priscilla had chatted on about Elspeth and Dougal and how she loved Fair-acre Valley. Finally she got round to her visit to the butcher's.

'Mrs Swallow gave me some mushrooms she'd just picked. If Barnabas doesn't make it for dinner, would they keep till tomorrow if I put them on the marble slab in the storeroom? He's so fond of them. Then I could ask him tonight if he'd come for dinner tomorrow night.'

Rosina seemed to gulp, swallow, clear her throat. Then she said, 'He isn't coming at all tonight, I'm afraid.'

Priscilla felt as if she'd missed a step in the dark. No, oh no, that couldn't be! Not after that phone conversation. Not after being away ten days. But she mustn't give too much away. She managed, 'Did he ring? Has something cropped up?'

'I—I expect so. Yes, that must be it. You know how it is when you've been away from a business as large as that. Work just stockpiles. Perhaps he's dining travellers.'

'Could be. So when *is* he coming?'

She heard Rosina swallow again. She didn't meet Priscilla's eyes. 'Well, he isn't. I mean, not this week, anyway. So we'll eat the mushrooms ourselves.'

'Not this *week*? But that's absurd. He——' What could she say? A whole week . . . and he'd been here two or three times a week ever since she'd been here. A very solicitous nephew, she'd thought, and so he was, but lately she'd dared to hope he'd come to see her, not only to work on the book at that.

Priscilla started again, 'He *must* be busy. But surely he'll pop out for an hour or two to see . . . you?'

Rosina said firmly, 'I've never expected him to dance attendance on me, I value my independence too much. But he knows what care you take of me, so I mustn't appear hurt.'

Priscilla said hastily, 'Of course not. It's just that he's been here so much, I was—a little surprised. Sure we'll have the mushrooms tonight. I'll make a special dish the children will like—a pancake with mushroom filling. And we'll fry the flounder fillets.'

Rosina said, 'I'll wash up if you want to have the afternoon on your book at Thistledown, Priscilla.' Priscilla had the distinct impression that Rosina didn't want to continue talking.

She'd never felt less like work, but went. Manuel's study had such a mellow atmosphere she felt it calmed her jangled nerves immediately. This was where she and Barnabas had worked together in complete accord. Here were the sketches, the typescript, his drawings on the wall, done with their delicacy of touch that had seemed so at variance with the business head she'd known at first. Here they had laughed together, quoted poetry, become obsessed with their own creation . . . here they had known their first kiss. The memory of it washed over Priscilla, bringing back its fleeting magic. How absurd to feel so flattened because he wasn't rushing out here. She'd read more urgency into his phone call than she should have, that's all.

Barnabas had a big business on his mind. No, Priscilla, you oughtn't to expect him to neglect things for you. He'll be so tired after his hectic stay up north. But a week? A week? Work was out of the question. An hour and a half yet before the children would be in, full of eagerness and questions, wanting their substitute mother. She must walk off her megrims, meet them with serenity. The hills were near. She set off.

She came back outwardly unchanged, inwardly full of

doubts. Nat came in, upset because he felt he must tell tales about Timothy. He'd gone off swimming with three other lads to a river pool where Barnabas and Rosina had expressly forbidden the Darfield children to go. It was full of snags and changed with every heavy fall of rain, so that no amount of familiarity with it was any protection. Barnabas had said it must be the school baths, under supervision, or nothing.

Nat said miserably, 'Tim'll be mad with me because the other boys said he was chicken. Tim got all snooty and said pooh, he'd been in that pool dozens of times and could even dive off the big willow, he'd show them who was chicken.'

'I'll think of something,' Priscilla promised him. 'But even suppose he sulks for days, I'd rather that than have him strike his head on a submerged log. Don't worry, Nat, it's over to you to see your younger brother doesn't come to harm.'

She was into the Mini and away. She'd no compunction about bending the truth to save Nat from Timothy's wrath. She'd say someone had told her he'd seen Tim and the Moffat boys making for the river. Just as she passed the store, out came Mr Moffat. She stopped. She'd have to risk him thinking her a fusspot. It was amazing how many parents allowed swimming in dangerous spots go unsupervised.

She liked Sam Moffat. He was a no-nonsense person. She told him what had happened, said, 'How do you feel about it?'

He came round to the passenger door, wrenched it open, said, 'Drive on. I'll let *them* know how I feel. We'll not let on about Nat, I'll say I heard in the store and asked you to get me there. Step on it!'

Afterwards Priscilla wanted to laugh. This was one of the moments when you were glad to have a man at hand. No bleating about the equality of the sexes. The moment the boys saw Sam they came out of the water. Tim was halfway up the big willow towards a branch that would have made his dive too deep. He scrambled down too in response to Sam's bellow. There were two Moffat boys and one other. Sam didn't know him, so he said, 'Get your clothes and get home—and I mean get home. I'll find out who you are and I'll ring your mother as soon as I get to a phone, so you'd better make a clean breast of it. Do your swimming in the school pool. What the devil do you think we raised all that money for if it wasn't to stop drownings? As for you two . . . come here!'

He spanked his sons, quickly and effectively. Tim got the shock of his life when Sam strode over to him, yanked him over his knee and delivered the spanking where the good Lord meant spankings to be. Tim yelled mightily.

Then Sam said, 'Now, get in beside Priscilla and no more of this. You ought to be ashamed of yourself. With your example before her, Alicia could have been in here next . . . and us sending cables to Papua for your parents to come back for her funeral. Priscilla, I'll march mine home, clean through the main street in their togs, so everyone knows they're in trouble and the rest of the kids coming away from the baths will know this sort of foolhardiness doesn't pay.'

Tim didn't speak all the way home. When he got out to open the gates and got back in, he looked shamefacedly at Priscilla, said, 'I'm sorry. It was a clottish thing to do. My dad thumped me once for taking a dare. He said it was weak, not brave. Don't tell them in a letter, will you, it'd worry them?'

'Fair enough. Over and done with.' As they drove into the garage she exclaimed, 'Merciful heavens, what's that?' Eldritch shrieks rent the air from the direction of the barn where Alicia and Nerolie had been peacefully writing their stories. Tim had an air of relief. If the girls were in trouble it would take the heat off him.

Priscilla sped to the barn to find Nerolie on her back, and Alicia, looking far from angelic for once, kneeling on her, slogging her—there was just no other word for it. Priscilla hauled her off, managing to get kicked on the shin while so doing. A torrent of accusations poured from both. Priscilla drowned them out by a mighty yell, and when they'd subsided, said in a deadly tone, 'I'm going to know the meaning of this, and if you two can't quarrel without a scene like this, you won't be allowed to play together for a week.'

Alicia had criticised Nerolie's story as being too, too incredible. No little girl would be as brave as her heroine, staying by herself in a forest and not being scared. Nerolie might think she'd written an exciting story, but Alicia's was true to life. Nerolie had replied that just because Alicia was a cowardy-custard herself, it didn't mean all girls that age were, and pooh, she'd think nothing herself of staying in a house with deep bush all around, even if lions and tigers and snakes and elephants were abounding! Whereupon Alicia had flung herself on Nerolie like the aforesaid tiger and said she was twice as brave as Nerolie because she could fight as well as any boy and Nerolie always ran away!

Finally, Priscilla said, 'If I take you home, Nerolie, your mother will probably agree with me that you're far too much in each other's pockets and that it'll be best for you to be separated for a time, so if you like to make it up, she needn't know, and you can go home at the usual time.'

Doubtfully they agreed to this and settled down, each at their own end of the table, but it couldn't be said that their afternoon together had been a success. Priscilla got Nat to walk Nerolie home. She had this wistful feeling that Barnabas just might ring up, and express regret that he was deluged with business, explain it a little. Rosina just might have got him wrong.

At five-thirty-five when the shop would have closed, she went up to the upstairs hall, looked longingly at the phone, then succumbed to temptation and dialled his number.

She was in luck, he answered it; that meant everyone had gone. When she said, 'Oh, Barnabas, it's Priscilla here,' there was a long pause. She said, 'Are you there, Barnabas? Can you hear me?' he just said, 'Yes,' and left her to go on from there.

His tone chilled her to the marrow. But now she'd made contact she must continue. She said, 'Rosina told me you won't be out for a week.' She waited. He said nothing and said it very eloquently. He might just as well have said: 'So what?'

How telling a silence could be! Telling in this way: that he simply didn't want to speak to her. But she must find out why, though not directly. She moistened her lips, said, 'Barnabas, if you're engulfed in a backlog of work can I be of any assistance? I could come in, help at the office, even bring some work back here.'

His voice was deadpan. She'd never heard it like that before. 'No, thanks, Priscilla. You aren't on the staff now, and I think it would be very unwise. Look, I'm staying back in an endeavour to catch up on things. I'm afraid I can't spare the time to——'

It was too much for Priscilla. She said savagely, 'Don't hang up. You can certainly spare the time for this. It won't take long. I'm through with you, through with you in any capacity whatever. You must be the most unreliable man emotionally I've ever had the ill-luck to meet! You can completely wipe our project. I'll create myself another character. From now on, if we have to meet for Rosina's sake, it won't mean a thing. You're quite, *quite* horrible, Barnabas. Goodbye!'

She put the phone down, glared at it, said in a fierce undertone to the instrument, 'And I'm damned if I'll cry over you. You aren't worth a single tear!' and walked straight into her room.

CHAPTER TEN

BY some superhuman effort she managed to control herself. All sorts of foolish dreams came crashing about her, those castles in the air . . . but there was the evening meal to get, Alicia's rumpled feelings to be restored to normal, Rosina's usual serenity to be protected. She mustn't know that Priscilla and Barnabas had actually come to words on the telephone. *She would not let this matter . . . or if that were impossible, she wouldn't let it show!*

Everyone else thought the mushroom pancakes served with ham delicious, but Priscilla might just as well have been eating leather. She did everything mechanically. She was glad when the children asked her to play ball with them. Alicia, she noticed with relief, wasn't moping about her fight with Nerolie. She didn't refer to it till Priscilla tucked her down, kissed her goodnight, then just as Priscilla went to walk out of the darkened room, she said, 'I told Nerolie before she went home that seeing she'd told such whoppers about her mother and father, I really couldn't believe in her stories either. They're too silly for words. *My* stories will be believed.'

Priscilla went back, sat on the bed, smoothed back the golden hair. 'Don't be too hard on her, love. Nerolie probably feels a bit silly about being found out. Let her give that imagination of hers free rein in her stories. It'll get it out of her system. Know what I mean?'

A long silence. 'I think so. Priscilla, I don't think I'll have my window open tonight. Would you mind shutting it?'

Priscilla smiled inwardly. She had an idea Nerolie's creepy stories really had scared Alicia. As she reached the door again, Alicia asked, 'When's Uncle Barnabas coming out? I miss him.'

'I've no idea. As soon as he can, I suppose.' Priscilla went downstairs. She knew Rosina was unhappy for her sake and this made her even madder with Barnabas. Not desolate, that would come later, just angry.

She made herself sound amused. 'Alicia is unrepentant. It probably won't hurt her and Nerolie to have a little spat now and then. They were too intense. It's also made Nerolie see she mustn't draw the long bow too much. I thought I was having the wisdom of Solomon in directing Nerolie's imagination into new channels, but it only provided fresh fuel for quarrels. I have a feeling they're educating me as much as I'm educating them.'

Rosina looked relieved at her light tone. 'That's what parenthood is all about. A sense of inadequacy sometimes saves us from being pompous.' Thoughts of Barnabas rushed back on Priscilla. How when she'd first heard of Rosina's nephew, the horrible Barnabas, she'd deemed him pompous. Well, perhaps he was, the lordly Barnabas, unbending enough to draw a girl on, then slamming a door in her face.

'Lovely to have a night to ourselves, I think I'll write Andrew,' said Priscilla. 'I've such a lot to tell him, Clarice and Roger being here, and how well they're getting on. Funny, but there's far more to write about in village life, too, than in town. He'll enjoy the story about me wondering how to handle Tim so he didn't lose face in front of his mates, and Sam Moffat just wading in and spanking them. I know what Andrew would say, lots of sound psychology in moderate spankings.'

'I was thankful you were here. You may not have known what to do, but you upped and offed and collected reinforcements on the way. I can see now it was this sort of thing Barnabas feared I'd not be able to cope with. You're the right age, so resilient.'

Priscilla reflected that she'd need to be as resilient as a rubber ball to bounce back after this. She wrote her letter, they looked at a play, sat up late, not wanting to lie awake and wonder. Finally Rosina yawned, looked hopefully at

Priscilla who promptly yawned too, to make her think she was sleepy, and said goodnight. Priscilla saw Rosina take a couple of aspirin, most unusual for her.

She wouldn't take any herself. She wasn't going to let that mercurial, unreliable Barnabas have any effect on her. She would take that new creepy mystery Rosina had got from the library, and lose herself in it. She would *not* have a white night agonising over Barnabas Lockhart. Life at Jesmond Dene wasn't for her after all. And she couldn't stand it without him. Well, she'd travel, do what Andrew had often asked, go to the other side of the world, and make a new life for herself. That was the thing to do . . . plan a whole new future . . . At the thought sheer desolation swept over her. An hour later she went along to the bathroom, took aspirin, and because she so rarely took anything like that, sank almost immediately into an engulfing sleep . . .

Nightmare succeeded the first merciful oblivion. In it she was alone, dreadfully alone and frightened. She didn't know why she was frightened, just that some nameless terror clutched her heart and paralysed her limbs. She needed help, but no help was forthcoming, because in all Fair-acre Valley there was no other living person left, and outside raged a terrible storm and no human succour could come to her. And it would be like this always, with no voice to break the solitude, no touch to warm her icy fingers . . . she struggled to wake, but her arms were pinned to her sides, she thought, and the only movement she could make was to turn her head ceaselessly from side to side.

She wanted to call for Barnabas, but what was the use, because Barnabas was never going to return. Then suddenly the tossing and tumult of the storm ceased and it was like a miracle, because into the stillness came the sound of a car. Lights, she dreamed, rayed up over her ceiling, the car stopped, the light went out, and she heard a car door open, a step on the gravel. She listened then with agonising strain for a house door to open, for her rescuer to come, but though she listened and listened, there were no other steps. Then presently, the car door shutting and that most dreadful sound of all, an engine starting, and the sound of a car retreating, till all sound ceased and again she was left in the grip of terror, alone.

Suddenly she came up to the surface of consciousness, knew it for nightmare, woke completely and sat up, trembling. Oh, how real nightmares were ... how wonderful it must be when married to have someone there to waken you, to summon you back from those strange regions in which you wandered, shake you, laugh tenderly, say, 'Darling, it's all right. It was just a nightmare,' and fold you close. Stop it, Priscilla! That's ridiculous. You'd better read.

An hour later, a little reassured, she snapped off her light. Immediately unease flooded her. That had been horrible, but sometimes real sounds intruded in dreams, in fact possibly caused them. There hadn't been a car, surely? Why would there be? Burglary was unknown in Fair-acre. Plenty in the nearby city, but this was such a tiny village, relic of pioneering days when swamp had made transport difficult, and the few shops had served the larger farming community, and had remained. Nothing to attract crime.

She got out of bed and went to her window, peering out under the eaves. She pulled back the purple drapes and instantly knew fear because away from the house, beyond the bridge, was to be seen something that meant her fears were justified ... a light in the Thistledown House. In fact, lights in the plural.

For a terrifying instant she felt turned to ice. Then her heart began to knock against her ribs. She put a hand out to each side of her, clutching at the window frames. 'Priscilla, don't panic. You've got to get help, from the village. It's just round the bend in the road. Use the phone.'

But she mustn't put her light on—it could be seen from here. Whoever had entered the chalet had come here first, gazed up at this dark house, gone out and back up the track to Thistledown. They must go on thinking no one stirred here.

She mustn't disturb Rosina if possible. But she must use the downstairs phone to summon help. That light wouldn't be seen. The phone was some distance from Rosina's room, there was a spare room and Alicia's before Rosina's. Pity there was no policeman stationed here, there hadn't been for years. But she could ring the Dunedin police and they'd act very quickly.

She felt round for her clothes. She mustn't waken the boys. They'd want to do something rash, for sure, but they slept like the dead. On went summerweight slacks, a loose top. She wished she'd had a cardigan out, but it had been hot and she wouldn't rootle around for one. She took another look before creeping downstairs. The lights were still on, one downstairs one and either the bedroom or the study. She felt sick at the thought of anyone among Manuel's treasures, Barnabas's exquisite drawings. There could be vandalism, even malicious arson. How terrible if all Rosina's dear memories of Manuel were reduced to ash!

Without a sound Priscilla reached the foot of the stairs. A passage led off to the other rooms. She didn't know what made her want to peep into Alicia's room. She'd listen for the child's breathing, assure herself she was deeply asleep.

She didn't listen after all, because as soon as she stopped in the doorway she knew something was wrong because a cool night wind struck on her face . . . and she had shut the window! She stood stock-still in the doorway and the room was quite light because the curtains were pulled back, and the moonlight shone in *on to an empty bed*. Priscilla's hand flew to her mouth to stifle her cry. She mustn't wake Rosina . . . yet.

She couldn't be in the bathroom, there was no light there. Besides, if Alicia got up in the night, she always put her own light on. Priscilla went in, closed the door, switched on the light. This couldn't be seen from the chalet, it was at the back of the house.

The clothes were flung back from the bed, Alicia's dressing-gown and slippers were gone. So was the Raggedy-Ann doll she still took to bed. Priscilla felt as if her stomach turned over. There had been that sound of the car, the lights on her attic ceiling . . . had it been a dream, or dread reality? Terror clutched her. Rosina had taken aspirin and would have slept soundly, so had she. Had someone taken Alicia? Taken her across to the chalet? At the thought, a scream rose in her throat but was choked back. She must, for Alicia's sake, get help from the village before she sped across to the chalet. Should she wake Rosina? No, she was past seventy. Her heart might not be strong. If she took a turn it would delay Priscilla in reaching Alicia, she must do what everyone did in Fair-acre when in doubt or trouble . . . ring the Manse.

Barnabas Lockhart had worked on at his office till ten-thirty. It was ridiculous, nothing had needed attention till that hour, but he hadn't wanted to go home to Tyne Hill, to a big house with just a housekeeper and gardener in their own quarters.

For more than thirty-six hours his thoughts had been torment. In vain he told himself Priscilla Marchant wasn't worth agonising over like this. He hadn't despised her that day in his office when that fellow Roger had come in and they'd gone into his sanctum and he'd heard the tail-end of their discussion when they'd decided to break off their affair. He'd given her the benefit of the doubt then, assured himself they'd broken it off *before they'd gone too far*. He'd admired them both.

That was why when she'd written, presumably from Christchurch, to say she was seeking a position there, he'd not been too upset, had thought it wise; then had been surprised to find in himself a sense of utter loss at her absence from his daily scene. He'd thought it might be pleasant to run up there some time, take her out, see her in a different setting.

What a shock he'd got at finding her at his aunt's and had known disillusionment at her deceit. Worst of all, facing up to the reason why ... it couldn't have been anything else but that after all, she couldn't say a complete goodbye to Roger. He'd later tried not to be too harsh ... had told himself she'd only wanted to stay near him, to be within reach of his voice by phone, for the occasional family visit. She might have intended the situation to remain at that, but it hadn't, had it? *A memorable weekend*, that bounder had said. Barnabas went over and over it. Rosina must have gone off for a weekend, possibly to her friend at Te Anau. No doubt Clarice had thought Roger away on a business trip. It had been too ideal for them ... an empty chalet in the larchwood, and himself in Christchurch, only the children in the house. Good God, had she left them there, sleeping alone in a wooden house? He'd tear strips off her if she had.

He got his car out of the shop car-park, gripped his wheel. He should have gone straight through the Octagon from Princes Street, to George Street and out on the Karitane Road to Tyne Hill. Instead he swung left, past the Robbie Burns statue and St Paul's Cathedral, and headed towards Three-Mile Hill and Fair-acre.

He wouldn't get these burning resentments, this slow, consuming anger out of him till he'd had it out with her; till he'd told her that though she'd hoped to keep him dangling, evidently, while she dallied with her sister's husband, it wasn't on. She was out of his life for good, and from Rosina's too.

But when he came to a stop outside the house not even an attic light showed. She was presumably sleeping the sleep, not of the just, but of the uncaring. He couldn't rouse the whole house by demanding admittance at this hour. And now he was here he knew he couldn't make a scene in front of Rosina at any time. He'd call Priscilla into town, and tell her what he thought of her there. He started up and drove away.

As he passed through the quiet village street, he saw a light on in Dougal's study; Dougal, his best friend. He wouldn't have to rouse a household here with a bell, he could tap at the French windows and go in.

Dougal opened the door, a little surprised, but not much because Manses were like that. It could have been a charming scene, Dougal evidently busy at his desk, till disturbed, Elspeth curled up in a shabby old wing chair, keeping him company. Barnabas envied him.

Elspeth sprang up, eyes alight, came to Barnabas, holding out her hands to him. 'Oh, Barnabas, you've come to tell us! You've just left Priscilla.' Then the eager words died on her lips as she saw the look on his face.

Barnabas said, 'I've not seen Priscilla since yesterday morning.'

Elspeth boggled. '*Yesterday* morning? But she never said. She was in here today, all eagerness for your return. She —I don't get it. Yesterday morning, what can you mean?'

'She didn't see me. I saw *her*.'

Dougal said, 'Sit down, Barney. I think you've had a shock. Sit down and tell us what's wrong.'

Barnabas sat down. Dougal motioned Elspeth to her chair, pulled his desk chair round between them. 'Now, what's the story?'

Barnabas hesitated. 'It was the oddest thing. I had reason to distrust her right from the time she took this job with my aunt. She was going on holiday. Her brother-in-law had come into the office to see her, didn't want to talk to her at home.'

'Naturally,' said Elspeth.

Barnabas frowned. 'You knew? She told you?'

'Yes. It was an awkward situation, wasn't it?'

'*Awkward?* That's the understatement of the year! I told them to go into the Sanctum, so I overheard a bit of it when they were coming out, and it was easy enough to put two and two together. So when I got a letter from her posted from Christchurch, saying she was looking for a job there, I admired her for it—admired them both. You can imagine how I felt when I found out that bit of deception . . . getting a friend to post it for her up there. Finding her at my aunt's was a devilish coincidence, for her. It was only because it was helping Rosina out that I didn't tell her to go there and then. It was obvious she couldn't, after all, find the resolve to break off the affair.'

A line appeared between Elspeth's brows. Dougal made a surprised sound. Elspeth said, 'Affair? What affair? What can——'

Barnabas stared. 'You said you knew. That she told you.' He sounded clean exasperated.

Elspeth said, 'She told me why she let you think she was going to Christchurch. Because of Melisande. Because she thought you were nearly engaged. Oh, Barney, you've got your wires crossed, just as Dougal and I did. Affair with whom?'

'With Roger, of course.'

Elspeth fell back against her chair. 'With Roger . . . her brother-in-law? You've gone mad, clean mad!'

'I wish I had. I wish it weren't true. I——'

Elspeth said, 'Priscilla and I had quite a a conversation at the gate this morning. I almost forced a confidence she wasn't prepared to give . . . yet. She was all a-star over Melisande meaning nothing to you, and obviously hoping your return meant something for her. She told me she'd given up her job because for months she'd been in the corny position of a secretary in love with her boss . . . you! And you were so obviously tied up with Melisande. She couldn't stand it any longer, so she was going away.

'She met Rosina, found she needed someone just like her, and because she thought she should get away from you altogether, that you'd think it odd if she took such a poorly paid job so near to Dunedin and would probably try to persuade to stay with you at least part time, sent you her resignation with a Christchuch address on it. A girl suffering from unrequited love is a proud girl, Barnabas. She'd have done anything to stop you guessing.'

When he stared at her unbelievingly she added, 'She even told me she'd never fallen in love before. She'd even thought of herself as a cold fish ... till she met you. So what's this nonsense about Roger? Whatever you overheard, it was ambiguous out of its context.'

Barnabas gave a short, disbelieving laugh. Dougal took over. 'Barney, that's right. We all say things with double meanings at times. If it had been like that I'm pretty sure you wouldn't have been allowed to hear a word of it. I'd stake my oath on Priscilla's integrity. It just can't be. Get that into your head.'

Again Barnabas gave the short laugh. 'I'm not just going on that. I came home a day early because I was so eager to see her I couldn't wait. I'd been waiting so long, for her to get Roger out of her system. I thought she was making a good effort, but I couldn't, in fairness to her, rush my fences. But we were so kindred, so right for each other ... it seemed too good *not* to be true. I intended going into the shop Monday morning, then thought to hell with business ... and took off for here thinking she'd just have got the children off to school, that only she and Rosina would be home. But Rosina's car was away, she must have gone away for the weekend, so I went across to the Thistledown House, on foot over the bridge, and there they were ... Priscilla and Roger, kissing a fond goodbye, and he thanked her for *a memorable weekend*! Now explain *that* away!'

He saw Dougal and Elspeth exchange glances that were more bewildered than shocked. Then Elspeth said, 'You *are* mad! Clean mad ... stark, staring, raving mad!'

Dougal said, some sort of light breaking over his face, 'Barney, there's been a gigantic mistake. Listen and listen carefully. *Rosina was here all weekend*. Got that? All weekend.' Barnabas's face showed no expression, just intentness. Dougal continued so slowly Elspeth could have shaken him. 'Roger *and* Clarice spent the weekend here. They were in church Sunday night. *They* occupied the bedroom in the chalet. It was quite a weekend party. Nerolie Palmerston stayed with Alicia. When Priscilla called in here after shopping this morning ... shopping for the makings of a meal in case you could come for dinner ... she said that as Roger was due in Invercargill today, to save him going back all the way to town with Clarice, Rosina took Clarice in. Rosina had nerines to deliver, and they went in early because Clarice had a man coming to cut the hedge at nine. I saw them myself dropping the kids at the school gates. So when you saw Roger kiss Priscilla and thank her for a memorable weekend, he meant memorable because he and his wife had been on their own for once—their children were away in Central Otago!'

Then Barnabas's face had so many expressions chasing over it, they could only gaze. The two main ones were delighted relief and remorse: He groaned. 'What am I going to do?' he demanded. 'No girl would have anything to do with a man who'd thought that of her when she was completely innocent. She was cutting enough last night when she thought I was just dropping her. She said I was the most unreliable man emotionally she'd ever had the ill-luck to meet. And so I am. But this—oh, Dougal, what a fool you must think me!'

Dougal said patiently, 'You said no girl would have anything to do with a man for thinking that of her, but it isn't true. You're looking at one right now. That's exactly what I thought of Elspeth.'

Barnabas's jaw dropped again. It would probably never be the same again, Elspeth thought, beginning to giggle. 'You must be clean mad,' said Barnabas, with a vague, unsatisfactory feeling that someone had said just that some time ago. 'Not of Elspeth ... why——'

'He did,' she giggled, 'all men are mad.'

Dougal said sternly, 'It was your own fault. You said the most ambiguous things, even wrote an ambiguous poem that made me sure. Look, no one knew the full truth of that mix-up. They only knew Elspeth had thought she couldn't marry a minister because she'd sheltered a criminal in her flat all night. The way she went on I thought she'd had an affair and was prepared to be all noble and forgiving. Barnabas, we don't deserve the women we get, but I'm sure you won't lose Priscilla. It's too right to stay wrong.' He looked at the study clock. 'Thunder and turf, you can't go along there now, you'd scare the life out of them. You'll just have to see her first thing in the morning. You said her light was out.' He grinned wickedly. 'Maybe she's not as upset as she might have been. Perhaps she doesn't think you worth worrying over. After all, she's got no guilt complex, so she probably thinks you are——'

Barnabas said, 'I told you what she thinks I am . . . the most unreliable man emotionally she's ever met. And quite, *quite* horrible to boot.'

Callously, Dougal began to laugh. 'Oh, man, you've sure blotted your copybook . . . but not to worry, it'll all come out in the wash. You're not going back to Tyne Hill. Ring your housekeeper in case they think you've had a smash and say you're staying here. Then you can see your fair Priscilla in the morning. As soon as you see the children arrive at school, you can take off for Jesmond Dene. Oh, boy, your aunt will just wipe the floor with you!'

Elspeth said, 'Stop that nonsense this moment, Dougal. I've a better idea. I'll ring her tomorrow morning and without giving her a chance to ask anything, I'll say I've a terrific emergency on, could she bring the kids to school and drop in here. You'll be in the drawing-room. I'll push her in and turn the key so she can't just slap your face and rush straight out again.'

Barnabas said, 'I've heard of Job's comforters before . . . how much better do you think this is making me feel?' Then he added, 'Oh, Elspeth, what's the matter?' as tears rushed to her eyes and spilled over.

'She was so happy,' she sobbed. 'She had a basket with some fillet steak in and Mrs Sparrow had given her field mushrooms, and I produced some flounder for an entrée . . .

she had stars in her eyes . . . Oh, I can't bear to think what she's been through.' She snatched at a hanky and mopped at her eyes.

Barnabas, appalled, stepped forward, seized her, folded her against him, said, 'Don't, Elspeth. Don't cry.'

'Watch it,' said Dougal. 'Had I been out tonight and walked in the glass doors, I'd probably have clocked you one . . . so you just remember that little scene with Roger and Priscilla was entirely innocent.'

'Well,' said Elspeth, sniffing, 'we can't do one damned thing about it till tomorrow morning. I'm going to make us some coffee and sandwiches and you're going to get off to bed, Barney. The sooner you get to sleep, the sooner morning will be here.'

Dougal said, 'I'll put the kettle on for you,' and followed her out of the room. They were just out the door when the phone rang. Dougal looked back. 'Answer that, Barney, before it wakes the kids up.'

Barnabas lifted the phone said, 'The Manse here, can I help you?' and nearly dropped the phone as Priscilla's voice in tones he'd never heard before said, 'Dougal, you must come here immediately. Alicia——' then she stopped and said in an anguished note, 'It's *not* Dougal. It's you, Barnabas. I must have rung your number. You're no good to me, you're too far away. I wanted the Manse, get off the line.'

He shouted her down, 'It *is* the Manse! For God's sake, Priscilla, what is it? I'm here. What——'

'It's Alicia,' said Priscilla. 'She's gone. She's nowhere in the house and her window is open and there's a light in the chalet. Someone's got her there—there was a car. I thought it was a dream. Get Dougal here!'

'We're both on the way. But the car was me—I wanted to see you. But the house was all dark. How can she be missing? Pris——'

'Just shut up,' she cried savagely, 'and get here. Come up *this* drive so they won't hear you and run off with her. I'll go over the bridge.'

He fairly bellowed through the phone, 'You stay right where you are till we get there. Priscilla, do you hear? *Stay where you are.* We won't be five minutes.'

Her voice went low and intense. 'I can't. Five minutes may be all she's got left. I'm going. *Now.* I'll take the fire-irons.'

Barnabas's face was chalk-white as he faced Dougal and Elspeth aghast in the doorway. It took just seconds to say what had happened. Dougal said to Elspeth, 'Wake Danny and tell him we've been called out to an accident and you follow us when you've done that. We're on our way. You might be needed for Rosina.' And he was running after Barnabas who was making for his car still in the street. There was a screech of tyres and they were gone.

Elspeth knew she could run like a hare ... that the garage was locked and it was a horrible drive to back down. She woke Danny, and flew out of the house and down the village street in the bright moonlight, still in her slippers.

Priscilla didn't waken Rosina, she was afraid of her reaction and that might delay her. Only Alicia mattered. Sweet Alice, so little, so dear. She seized the fire-tongs, heavy and huge, and sped out, heading for the path to the chalet.

She had a feeling she was going to go berserk, and when she came to grips with whoever it was, she'd yell her head off ... noise, that was her best ally. The intruder, kidnapper, whatever he was, couldn't know who slept in the house, how many could come in response to screams. Priscilla, like Elspeth, could run like a hare.

She knew she'd have to slow up when she got near, creep in to take them unawares, try for a moment of surprise to give her the advantage. Alicia must be here, she *must,* oh, dear God, let her be here and unharmed. . . .

Over the bridge, through the larch wood, her slippers made no sound, but soon she must stop pelting, control her breath, save it for yelling.

The picket gate was unlatched, no sound there. She was

creeping now, thankful for the moonlight that showed her where to put her feet, because no snapping twig must give her away. Her ears strained. No cry from the chalet, no sound of movement.

She saw a vertical line of light ... the front door was ajar. Good, because it meant she would make no noise getting in, but she must remember that Barnabas had said the stairs creaked ... she'd have to mount them on the outside of the treads. She put her foot on the first. No creak. Slowly she made it. Two did creak, and she paused each time. Not a sound. Could Alicia be gagged? Was someone in that bedroom listening even as she was listening? She gained the landing, paused, drew in silent breaths to steady her, nerve her, inched along and part of the bed came into view. Someone had been in it. It was turned down, even looked as if it had been tossed back. The pillow was dented. There was a Raggedy-Ann doll lying across it. Dear God ... where was Raggedy-Ann's owner? Priscilla gripped the fire-tongs more tightly ... was someone behind the door, perhaps holding a hand over a small mouth? She'd have to rush right in and turn quickly.

She rushed, her impetus carrying her right across the room before she could swing round ... and when she did, the room was empty.

It was worse, much worse, than finding anyone. She flung open the wardrobe door, yanked up the bedspread, looked under the bed, rushed out into the study, banging switches down, then pell-mell down the spiral, across the big room and up the other, into those bedrooms. Nothing to show Alicia had been here save Raggedy-Ann.

Distraught, Priscilla began calling as she rushed out into the night. Noise wouldn't matter now, but if Alicia were out there in the darkness, escaping from someone, she might hear her, call back, or the sound might cause whoever was responsible to flee. Over and over she called her name in a frenzy.

She saw the lights of a car turn the bend of the lane, ray up, curve into the drive, come past the house almost to the bridge and realised they must have the windows down and have heard her, because they weren't bothering to be quiet. They could see her torch sweeping to and fro as she ran into the chalet garage, the summerhouse, the shed, calling, calling.

Barnabas reached her first, clutched at her, brought her against him, saying, 'Wheesht, wheesht . . . quiet now, my darling. We'll find her. Oh, my love, my love.' She suddenly went limp. He said urgently, 'Priscilla, don't pass out on me. Not now.'

She said, reviving, and with indignation, 'I've never fainted in my life!'

'Good girl! Darling, it's all right between us. I misjudged you on something. And we'll find Sweet Alice. Ah, Dougal, now, let's hear what happened. Darling, you did take it in that the car was mine, not a kidnapper's? Now . . . tell us.'

She told them, her breath coming in gasps. They went into the chalet, up to the bedroom. They felt so baffled. Nothing but the silent testimony of Raggedy-Ann.

Dougal said, 'We've got to get help. Rosina and the boys will have to know. Surely they're not still sleeping? Thank God Elspeth's coming any moment. She can look after Rosina.'

Barnabas said, 'She must be sleep-walking. There's no reason for anyone to kidnap Alicia. At least——' he checked. They all had the same thought. No reason, but what if an unbalanced mind, beyond reason, was responsible? He said savagely, 'Let's *think*. Was anything on her mind to make her sleep-walk? Has she been in trouble at school, or home?'

'No, Tim was in trouble, but Sam Moffat walloped him and Tim said he was sorry. But not Alicia—except she was thumping Nerolie when I got back.'

'What for?'

'A stupid quarrel over some stories they were writing. Nothing serious.'

'Then let's get back to the house. We've got to get a search party out. Dougal, that'll be your department. You'll know everybody. Priscilla and I will search together. You'll have to phone and delgate someone—the first person you phone—to rouse the others. If we don't find her extremely soon it will have to be the police. In fact, I think we should get them first. Come on, back to the house.'

Barnabas took Priscilla's hand and they began to run, Dougal in the lead. An old jingle was beating through Priscilla's brain, 'Alice, where art thou? Alice, where art thou?' until she could have screamed.

They reached the front steps and at that moment, into the pool of moonlight, from the bend in the drive, came two figures, hurrying but not running. Elspeth's and a smaller one—Alicia's! Priscilla thought it was some mental mirage conjured up by the stress ... because this Alicia was carrying a Raggedy-Ann!

Dougal and Barnabas croaked: 'Alicia?' and Elspeth said in a strange, husky voice, as if trying not to make too much of it, 'She's been taking Nerolie home. Nerolie was too scared to go herself. I came on foot and found her ahead of me. She must have come out of Palmerstons' gate about thirty seconds before I reached there.'

Barnabas felt Priscilla give a convulsive shudder, drew her to him with one arm and squeezed her. She got the message: Bear up, Elspeth didn't want them to dramatise things too much. Barnabas looked down on the small dressing-gowned figure and his voice wobbled. 'Alicia, please tell us exactly what happened?'

Priscilla felt a wave of love for Barnabas roll over her because his voice had wobbled. She rubbed her face against his sleeve. He looked down briefly and she saw the side of his mouth lift, and knew everything was right, gloriously, wonderfully right.

In the strange unearthly light of the moon they saw Alicia lift that purely concave little face of hers up towards them, and she began in her precise little voice, 'Nerolie was mad with me because I said the little girl in her story would have been scared to death in the hut in the forest. She was so mad, she decided to sneak off here and spend an hour or two at the chalet—she knows where the key's kept. She said it was fun at first. She brought some sausage rolls and some pop. And her Raggedy-Ann.

'Then she was going to knock on my window ever so gently and tell me what she'd done and go home and get into bed and nobody else would ever know. Then the wind sprang up and it got spooky. She'd just decided to go back home and not waken me but leave her Raggedy-Ann to prove she'd done it, but when she got outside she saw a car come up the drive. A man got out, an enormous man, and stood there looking at the house, then he got back in and went away. Did you ever hear such nonsense? It's her imagination again.

'She was terrified he'd be waiting for her round the bend, so she came and tapped on my window.' Alicia's voice took on a smug note. 'She was just about gibbering with fright. And she was scared she'd get walloped if I woke you up to take her home. She said you'd be so flaming mad, Priscilla, you'd wade right into her. Would you have?'

'I would,' said Priscilla.

'So there was only one thing to do. I got out of bed and walked her home. There wasn't any dew and I had my slippers on. She cried all the way home. But she got in without anyone knowing, through the door she'd left open.'

Barnabas felt Priscilla sag within the circle of his arm. He said swiftly, in a whisper as he tightened his grip, 'I'll never forgive you if you faint now. I'm determined I'll propose to you before daylight.'

She said, 'I'll faint if I like, but don't forget to propose when I come round, will you? I'm extremely curious to know what stopped you before.'

'Don't. You're going to be mad with me. Dougal and Elspeth think I'm going to have my face smacked, but it won't make any difference, you're going to marry me just the same.'

'That's good,' said Priscilla.

Dougal enquired, 'What are you two whispering about?'

Alicia said, 'Well, I expect they're saying I ought to go to bed now. My, I'm glad nobody's cross, and I'm tired. So's Raggedy-Ann.'

They trailed up the steps, and with the promptness of a stage cue the light came on and Rosina's voice said, 'What in hell's going on?'

No one answered ... so much to tell ... so many to take up the tale, then Alicia said in shocked tones, 'Aunt Rosina, you swore!'

Barnabas laughed, 'Aunt Rosina, you've missed the show of your life. Elspeth, take Alicia off to bed and tuck her in, I doubt if Priscilla's legs would carry her.'

Rosina flung open the drawing-room door with a magnificent gesture as Elspeth led Alicia off. 'In there with you,' she said.

There was a silence. They might all have been schoolchildren, caught in a gang prank and answerable to a schoolmaster. Elspeth came back, took one look at them and collapsed into irresistible laughter, all save Rosina. 'I am not amused,' she informed them in a Queen Victoria voice.

'You will be,' gasped Dougal, 'you will be. What we've been through this night! Talk about anti-climax. But thank God it *is* that way. Given another ten minutes and half the police force in Dunedin would've been bearing down on us and we'd never have lived down the subsequent blaze of publicity! Barnabas, how *would* you have explained your midnight vigil under Priscilla's window?'

Priscilla took a seat very suddenly. 'Then I didn't just dream it? And you did say on the phone it was you, but I couldn't take it in. And it wasn't a figment of Nerolie's imagination?'

Barnabas looked brazen. 'I'd come out to propose to you.'

Dougal said, 'What a lie! You'd come out to blast her ears off.'

Barnabas said bitterly, 'You'd never think you were my best friend, you whited sepulchre!'

Rosina stopped looking cross with them, and began to smile. 'Go on, nephew. I find this very interesting.'

Barnabas sat down on the arm of Priscilla's chair, took her hand, began to look down on her and smile. Dougal said, 'Man, you'll never get away without a full explanation to your aunt. Get it off your chest, then we'll let you propose to her.'

'You've ruined it,' said the poor bedevilled Barnabas. 'It would be bad enough to explain when—if ever—I get her to myself. Remember what you and Elspeth planned, Dougal? You were going to get Priscilla into the drawing-room at the Manse at nine tomorrow morning and lock us in. Now look what you've done.'

Elspeth's eyes were shining. 'If you men go on like this you'll never get it sorted out! Priscilla, Dougal and I got our wires badly crossed too. We could have parted irrevocably. Fortunately it came to a showdown. You know I thought I was no bride for a minister, because of that newspaper publicity? Well, that wasn't all. I was so ambiguous in my statements to Dougal, he thought I'd been living with a business friend of mine.

'History now begins to repeat itself, in your case. When Roger came to see you about the need for Clarice to stand on her own feet, Barnabas heard only a sentence or two at the last. I think you'd opened the door. Something about you ought never to have let it get this far. He thought you'd fallen for each other, and were breaking it up.'

Priscilla boggled. 'Roger? Roger and me?'

'Yes. He admired you for it. When you were away he missed you horribly and when he got your letter posted from Christchurch, made up his mind he'd visit you up there. Imagine what construction he put on it when he found you at Rosina's!'

Priscilla looked bewildered. 'What *did* he think ... beyond calling me a liar?'

'That you couldn't bear, after all, to put as much distance as that between yourself and Roger.'

Priscilla blinked, trying to take it in.

'So he decided to give you time to get over him. You, of course, thought he was tied up with Melisande. He didn't care because he didn't want to court you properly before you got Roger out of your system.' She was smiling now.

Priscilla turned to look up at Barnabas on the arm of her chair. 'But he was never in my system. There was never anyone till——'

He smiled down on her, 'I know, my love. I know now. Elspeth told me ... in a few glorious sentences that turned my world right way up again.'

Elspeth said hurriedly, not wanting to lose the thread of her story, 'It's all right. He knows now why you left his employ. I had to tell him because——'

Barnabas took over. 'She had to tell me because I called on them at midnight, absolutely distraught. You see, Priscilla, I came back Sunday and rushed out here Monday morning to see you. I saw Rosina's car away, thought she must have gone off for the weekend, and I hoped to find you at work at Thistledown House, and have you on your own. I belted over and was just emerging from the larchwood when you and Roger came out with his suitcases and he kissed you and thanked you for a memorable weekend!'

Priscilla fell back in her chair. 'Barnabas! What horrible timing!'

He nodded. 'And it's no use you flying into a rage and telling me what you think of me for thinking such a thing, because I don't care. You could lay me out with that fire-iron you were brandishing at the chalet at one o'clock this morning and I'd come to and tell you that you were going to marry me even if I have to stick a pistol in your ribs to get you to the altar!'

Priscilla took another look at him and burst out laughing, 'Oh, Barnabas, Barnabas, darling horrible Barnabas, what a proposal! But it doesn't matter. I'm accepting you here and now.'

'Cheers,' said Rosina. 'Now for heaven's sake, let's have a good strong cup of tea. I can't celebrate an engagement in champagne at this hour of the morning!'

It was all of an hour and a half before Rosina yawned and said she'd go back to bed. The five happy people had finished up by cooking bacon and eggs, laughing and planning, talking things over. 'I'll never forgive you if you get married at St Adrian's,' Dougal had said. 'Mr Smith can assist with the service, but it must be here. You belong to Fair-acre Valley in a very real way, Priscilla.'

'Of course it'll be St Enoch's,' she said. 'And Elspeth will be my matron-of-honour and Sweet Alice my flower-girl. Oh, I feel like the old lady . . . Lawks-a-mussy-can-this-be-I? A few hours ago I was the most miserable being in Fair-acre Valley.'

'No,' said Barnabas, 'that was me.'

That was when Rosina decided to go to bed. 'Maybe I'll not sleep, but I shall lie and feel how happy Manuel would be to know that I can live out my days in the Thistledown House, just as he planned, with these two dear children close to me.' She smiled wickedly. 'I've a feeling the newly-engaged couple will find better things to do than catch up on sleep. Poor things, they've not had much chance till now.'

Priscilla didn't even blush. She looked at Barnabas with serene confidence. Elspeth and Dougal rose, said their good-byes.

Barnabas said, 'Dawn is nearly here. Look out of the window. We'll watch it together from the bridge. You get that glimpse through the cleft in the trees, to Saddle Hill, and you know that beyond it the sun is rising over the Pacific, to waken the world, our new, fair world.'

Darkness was still embracing the shadowy valley as they walked towards that bridge over which they'd run in such terror for Alicia a few hours before. Now they walked hand-in-hand, planning a future. Their Lady-of-the-Fuchsias was happily planning for them too, they knew.

Barnabas said, 'I've got that love-letter I wrote you in Christchurch still in my pocket. After the sun comes up we'll go into Manuel's study and you shall read it. I've so many things to tell you. Priscilla, how *did* I contain myself? So often my feelings for you nearly overwhelmed me. I felt I couldn't expect you to shut one man out of your life and turn to me in a matter of weeks ... but now all this is ours ... the years ahead, working together on the thing nearest our hearts. Just imagine, love, *our* children will read of *Ambrosina*, not just generations of other people's children. Here's the bridge. Don't you think I've been a very patient man this last ninety minutes? Priscilla, the sun's coming up over the horizon and you are about to be kissed as you've never been kissed before ...'

He bent his head.

Harlequin's
Collection
EDITIONS OF 1979

YESTERDAY'S LOVE
FOR ALL YOUR TOMORROWS

You relive your love in memories. Letters tied in blue ribbon... roses pressed between the pages of a book... keepsakes of a romance that will never be forgotten.

A great love story has a different kind of timelessness. It can be cherished in memory, but it can also come alive over and over again. Harlequin proved that three years ago, when we introduced the first 100 Collections—outstanding novels, chosen from two decades of beautiful love stories. Stories that are still treasured by the women who read them.

Now we are bringing you the Harlequin's Collection editions of 1979. Best-selling romantic novels that were written from the heart, giving them a brilliance that the passage of time cannot dim. Like a lovingly crafted family heirloom or a gift from someone you love, these stories will have a special personal significance. Because when you read them today, you'll relive love. A love that will last, for all your tomorrows.

$1.25 each

Choose from this list of classic Collection editions

Relive a great romance...
Harlequin's Collection 1979
Complete and mail this coupon today!

Harlequin Reader Service

In U.S.A.
MPO Box 707
Niagara Falls, N.Y. 14302

In Canada
649 Ontario St.
Stratford, Ontario, N5A 6W2

Please send me the following Harlequin's Collection novels. I am enclosing my check or money order for $1.25 for each novel ordered, plus 49¢ to cover postage and handling.

☐ 152	☐ 161	☐ 169
☐ 153	☐ 162	☐ 170
☐ 154	☐ 163	☐ 171
☐ 155	☐ 164	☐ 172
☐ 156	☐ 165	☐ 173
☐ 158	☐ 166	☐ 174
☐ 159	☐ 167	☐ 175
☐ 160	☐ 168	☐ 176

Number of novels checked @ $1.25 each $ _____

N.Y. and N.J. residents add appropriate sales tax $ _____

Postage and handling $ _____ .49

TOTAL $ _____

NAME _____
(Please Print)

ADDRESS _____

CITY _____

STATE/PROV. _____

ZIP/POSTAL CODE _____

ROM 2281

Offer expires December 31, 1979

Harlequin Presents...

The beauty of true romance...

The excitement of world travel...

The splendor of first love...

unique love stories for today's woman

Harlequin Presents...
novels of honest,
twentieth-century love,
with characters who
are interesting, vibrant
and alive.

The elegance of love...
The warmth of romance...
The lure of faraway places...

Six new novels, every
month — wherever
paperbacks are sold.